THE TAX MAN

James Fischer

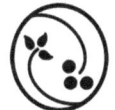

First published 2025
by Rowanvale Books Ltd
The Gate
Keppoch Street
Roath
Cardiff
CF24 3JW
www.rowanvalebooks.com

A CIP catalogue record for this book is available from the British Library.
ISBN: 978-1-83584-100-6
eBook ISBN: 978-1-83584-101-3

Dedicated to my parents, who I love very much.

CHAPTER 1

Often, David found himself at Stow Lake, nestled within San Francisco's Golden Gate Park. He would go there to reflect after a long, grinding day at work. The lake held some answer he couldn't quite grasp yet, thus he returned to it as frequently as he could, just to think, to be one with the still waters.

San Francisco in 1996 was chaotic and pulsing with energy. It was racing toward a newer age, the old-world charm falling behind as more modern structures were built. But David felt adrift in a city that was indifferent toward him. He didn't care, and the city reflected this like a mirror – no one really cared about him either.

Stow Lake, however, was different. It wasn't burdened by the same kind of frantic aliveness the city emanated. The foggy skies above were mirrored by the calm surface of the water, creating in David's mind the idea of an almost mythic stillness. The lake had this uncanny quality to it. Something haunting, promising to everyone who lingered too long that they would become bound to it, one way or another.

To David, the lake was a projection of his thoughts. Sometimes too deep to fathom, murky and elusive. There, time moved differently. It blended into itself, slipped away as he sat on a bench or leaned on the stone bridge. It could have been half an hour, could have been half a century; that wouldn't change the lake's history, just make him a part of it – unfortunately for him, as he would soon find out.

David's life wasn't what it should be. He was forty, expecting more clarity, more control and more stability. But his mind was like a fogged-up mirror. His self-reflection was blurry and clouded by doubt; his memory had become unreliable, fragments of his days slipping beneath the surface of consciousness without explanation.

His moments of anger were worse still. Whenever pressure built up inside him, be it from work, the hurdles of married life, or even from trying to relate to himself and inevitably turning to self-hate, he would spin into a blinding rage where he couldn't recall what was said or what had happened, leaving behind wrecked rooms and slammed doors, and his wife, the love of his life, the guardian of his heart and soul, Sarah, trembling in silence.

And then there was the lack of sleep. If he finally managed to drift off, usually in the early morning hours, it did not feel restful. He'd feel the sensation of sinking into a dreamless abyss, a black void that would erase the hours, but leave him feeling just as lost and just as heavy when he woke up, as if he was trying to grasp his way out of a tar pit.

But Stow Lake never judged him. It was eternal and unchanging, holding on to his secrets.

David had just gotten home from work. Another grueling day at the factory. He could see that there was some mail in his letterbox.

"Not again…"

It was a couple of advertising leaflets for pizza stores and wine and cheese places he couldn't afford. And then came the letter he dreaded most – the letter from the tax man.

"*Dear David,*" it began. "*We hope this finds you well. Our records indicate that you have an outstanding balance for 1995 and 1996 of six thousand dollars for each year…*"

Then there was some more bureaucratic babble, including the method he should use to pay his outstanding balance. There was only one problem. He didn't have the money.

Sarah hadn't come home yet and he was worried about her whereabouts; she was usually home cooking up some microwave dinner by this time, but he figured that she might be out with a friend and would return at some point later, maybe just before bed.

He tossed the letters on the kitchen table, which was covered with a plastic tablecloth patterned with faded flowers, opened up the fridge and did what any man would do in his situation: crack open a beer and hope that the world would just disappear for a while.

His chief worry was that they might come to take the house away from him. They might impose some fines or something like that, take his honest living away, who knew – he didn't know how these things worked. All he knew was that some bureaucratic bastard was on his case. Hard.

A few hours later, Sarah still hadn't come home, but sure enough, there was a ring of the bell. Had she forgotten her keys? Maybe she'd lost them. But he stopped himself as he saw the silhouette behind the window panes on the door. The form was too broad, too tall. That wasn't Sarah.

David put the chain on the latch and creaked the door open, just enough to see who it was without allowing them to barge in.

"Who are you?" he asked, a mixture of suspicion and slight nervousness in his voice.

"I'm Agent Carter," replied the man. He was wearing a suit and tie, and there was something sly about his tone that David didn't take too kindly to. "Uh – tax authority."

Damn it, thought David. He had to let him in – he had no other choice; this was a government agent.

"Alright, you can come in."

"Thank you very much – uh – David, isn't it?"

"That's right. My name's David."

"Thanks for welcoming me into your home. I hope there's nothing important going on that I might be interrupting?"

"Oh no, just waiting for the wife to come home," said David nervously.

Agent Carter took a good look around: the yellow-stained fridge, the rusty interior of a shabby home. David couldn't get much better than this – and Agent Carter knew this so well that it sparked a little hint of irony in him, because David didn't have the money.

"So, I suppose we sit down now and you talk to me about the ramifications of not paying my taxes for the past two years?"

said David, catching the peculiar little half-smile on the agent's face, his judgment of the house's shabby interior.

The agent pointed David to his kitchen table, as if he owned it. "Let's just take a quick seat over here."

Carter wiped the faded floral tablecloth with the sleeve of his suit, brushing away any dust or crumbs, and placed his briefcase on the table.

"So, uh, David," began Carter, taking a few brown files out from his briefcase. "This is what's going to happen. If you can't pay your taxes within the next twenty-four hours, we're talking about asset seizure here, pal. You ever hear about asset seizure?"

"I can't say I have, no," said David, hating how simple he sounded.

"That means we, the tax department, come here, into your lovely house, and we take anything we like. Anything valuable. You got a pretty decent car outside, maybe we could take that."

"Well, if you take my car, how am I supposed to get to work?"

"That's your problem, I'm afraid."

"Here's the deal, agent. I just don't have the money. So, isn't there a nicer way we can deal with this, rather than taking my car away from me?"

"I'm afraid that's the only option."

David looked at the clock on the wall: quarter past eight. He was growing more concerned about Sarah and just wanted this tightly strung dipstick out of his face so he could spend the evening with his wife. He just needed to accept what was being said and find some other means of transportation to get to work, maybe take the bus or train or something. That could be possible. Yeah.

"Well, alright, sir. I suppose if it needs to be that way it needs to be that way – doesn't it?"

Agent Carter was looking at David very intensely. "So it was that easy?" he asked in a low, mellow tone.

David perked up – it seemed this man would actually be leaving his house as soon as possible. "Yep!"

"Interesting..." said Carter contemplatively, making his way into the living room.

"Excuse me, agent. The door's that way."

"I'm not leaving yet," said Carter, his monotone oddly sickening to listen to.

David, a man of simplicity, simply replied, "Not leaving? Well, my wife's on the way home and we gotta cook dinner."

"Sit down," said Carter. "We aren't done yet."

David scratched his head in frustration. "Well, what else is there possibly to talk about? Oh, wait a minute, I get it. You want to know how I'll pay my taxes in the future, don't you? Well, don't you worry, sir, I'll make a budget, hold on to some cash real tight, do right by the law in the future."

"Future?" said Carter. "No such thing as future. All we have is now."

"You've been reading one too many self-help books," replied David, who wasn't fooling around anymore. "Now, get the hell out of my house."

"David, I find you to be a very interesting man."

David sighed. "What?"

"How long have I been here for?" Carter demanded.

"I don't know."

"Seven minutes. I've been keeping track of time on my watch. Seven minutes." Something that was not quite a smile worked its way onto Carter's face. "And I have to say, these have been the most important seven minutes of my entire life."

David could feel his pulse quickening. What could this man possibly mean by that?

"Look, I'm not looking for any trouble, sir, so please, if you don't mind, can you just leave?"

"But you've compelled me to stay! I'm magnetically drawn to this household, to you, to your wife who hasn't come home yet, to your job at the factory! Couldn't we just talk for a little while? Just you and me?"

David fumbled around. "T-talk? You want to talk? Well, alright, what do you want to talk about?" As previously stated, a very simple man indeed. "And how do you know I work at a factory?"

Carter sighed. "Uh, I'm a government agent. And you, David. I want to talk about you."

"What about me?" He was perplexed. Was this an invitation into a friendly conversation? Some kind of interrogation? What was going on?

Carter could see the desperation in his eyes. He slapped David on the knee. "Oh, relax, Dave. Just think about it this way – tonight, uh, it's just us pals here having a meaningful conversation about life."

"Well, where do we start?"

"We start with you."

"Why me?"

"Because you are the epicenter of your own universe!" said Carter triumphantly.

David's eyes remained dull. "And what does that have to do with anything?"

Carter was shocked. Hurt even. "What does that have to do with anything? That's your reaction? How could that possibly be all – don't you care about yourself? About anything? About your life?"

"No," said David. "The only thing I care about is whether I'm having mashed potatoes or boiled vegetables tonight. So, if you wouldn't mind getting the hell out of my house, that would be lovely."

"You see, this is what I hate," said Carter, raising his voice. "You've been twelve thousand dollars overdue for the past two years, I come here – in good faith – as a man who, uh, genuinely wants to help you, and you, being the bum that you are, you let me down like that? You let me down that hard? To my face? Just like that? Boiled vegetables or mashed potatoes? Are you serious, man? That's what you care about so deeply right now?"

"Look, pal, I just want my wife to come home. That's all. I didn't mean nothing by it, I didn't want to be a downer – maybe you have something to say. Alright, I get it, maybe you're concerned about me. Is that what the case is here?"

"You are my primary concern," he said, stiffening up and meeting David's eyes.

David chuckled. "You're a weird guy. You know that, right?"

"Weird? What's so weird about wanting to explore another human being's mind? Do you have a mind? Or are you really just some idiot who comes and goes from his house to the factory?"

"Hey, I find that quite insulting, Agent Carter, I'm not going to lie. But no, you're right, I do have a mind of my own, a soul, a personality – what is this, anyways? A therapy session?"

"By the end of this conversation, both you and I will certainly be in a better place – liberated, even. That, I can assure you."

"Right. Right. Of course. Yeah, I see what you mean. You just want an insight into how my mind works because you want to be friends? You want to know why I can't pay my taxes, if it's my personal life or my spending habits? What? What are you talking about, man?"

Carter was getting increasingly frustrated. He balled up his fists and exhaled loudly. "You are the epicenter of your own universe. Go back to that. Now. And tell me, what is the most important thing in your life? And if you say mashed potatoes or boiled vegetables one more goddamned time, I don't know what might happen between the two of us."

David found himself quite taken aback by this. This stranger, this man, this bureaucratic, pen-pushing, suit-and-tie man had invited himself into his house and wanted to know about the innermost workings of his mind?

"Sarah?" said David.

"Your wife."

"Yeah."

"Good. Now we're getting somewhere. What about her?"

"What about her? Well, I love her."

"You love her?"

"Yeah, I love her."

Carter smiled a big, warm, ironic smile. "You love her… That is touching. That is – uh – profound…Thank you, David…Thank you for sharing that with me."

"Sir, is there something going on with you?" asked David, perplexed. "Some kind of a break-up, maybe a divorce you're facing?"

"No."

"No?"

"I'm not married."

"Girlfriend, then?"

"No."

"Okay." This was growing troublesome for David; he couldn't keep up.

"So, you love Sarah, that's great. What else?"

"She wants kids, I don't. I don't want to bear the responsibility. I'm not in the financial position to have them anyway – you know that, don't you, Mr. Carter?"

"It's *Agent* Carter. Please address me properly next time."

"Sorry."

"So, you can't reproduce?"

"No, I can, I just don't want to."

"Your situation has rendered you impotent."

"Well, that's not the most polite way to say it, but I guess so, yeah."

"What if something bad ever happened to Sarah? What then?"

"Can we change the topic? I don't want to think about that," he said, and looked at the clock with a frown.

A smile emerged on Carter's face. "Sure, let's change the discussion. What else is going on in your little universe? Oh – uh – the factory. Yeah, tell me about your pathetic life at the factory."

"Pathetic life at the factory? Excuse me, sir, who the hell do you think you are?"

"So, it's not a pathetic, miserable existence? You like your life there, you like your job there, you like what you do?"

"It's an honest living."

"What is it exactly you do?"

"We recycle plastic."

"You recycle plastic? Then you should know more, surely, about how one thing turns into another, slowly, and over time its lifespan elapses and then it is reformed. Reborn?"

There was tension in the air. David was losing patience. "Reborn? What're you trying to say? Because I'm trying to put the pieces of this puzzle together and I just can't do it. You come into my house demanding money and assets and now you're talking about rebirth? Because I recycle...plastic?"

Carter inhaled deeply. Slowly. "Twelve thousand dollars overdue."

"I told you, I'll budget it out next time!"

"The twelve thousand dollars aren't the point!" shouted Carter. "It's you, man! It's always been you!"

"Okay, I think we're probably going to be here all night. I sure as hell don't know when Sarah's coming home, so do you want a cup of coffee, Agent Carter?"

"That would be lovely, David, thank you."

"Okay...*weirdo*," he mumbled under his breath and got up from the table.

"What if something was to happen to Sarah?" Carter persisted as David was heating up the water. "Say, she might be in danger? Someone tries to rob her? Maybe worse?"

"Stop goddamn talking about my wife like that!"

"I'm just catastrophizing. I know I'm a bureaucrat, but I have feelings too, you know, an imagination of my own. Sometimes, uh, it goes to the worst-case scenario."

"Oh, so now you're giving me an insight into *your* mind, okay, your own little epicenter bullcrap."

"Don't you want to know what it's like being me? Don't you care about anything at all?" asked Carter, as if he was unravelling a ball of wool.

"To be honest, I don't really give a damn about you, Carter. You know what I've realized? I've realized you just keep the anxiety at bay with your weirdo attitude. With you here, I don't need to worry about Sarah coming home, so here's your goddamn coffee. I hope you take sugar because I've put some in there for you, and I would love to hear you speak about yourself – go ahead."

"No, you don't need to worry about Sarah."

"Excuse me?"

"No, come on, let's talk about me. You know who I am. Agent Carter. I'm the investigative type. The more I know about a person the more I enjoy myself. And the fact that your car is going to be seized is rather, shall we say, funny to me. Twelve thousand dollars overdue…"

"Look, do you *know* me or something? Have we met before, maybe sometime in the past, and I just can't remember? Because you just seem to have a personal vendetta against my entire existence, don't you?"

Carter slurped on his coffee, and let out a gasp of pleasure. "A personal vendetta against your existence? That's what you think this is about?"

"Well, figuratively speaking, yes."

"Only figuratively?"

"Yes."

"Very good. Now we're getting somewhere. Do you want to go for a drive in the car? I mean, you only have one more day to use it, maybe we can go look for Sarah?"

"A drive?"

"A drive and a watchful eye, as we continue this lovely conversation. What model is your car anyway?"

"It's a Ford Tempo."

"Ah, just like everything else about you – it's got character, it's worn and torn, it's…devoid of meaning."

David felt like he had to tread carefully around Carter; there was something about him. They got inside the Ford, and David revved up the engine for what would be, according to Carter, the last time.

He drove past Sarah's usual go-to places: some coffee shops, clothes shops and so on. But she was still missing, a ghost in the night.

"What a shame," said Carter. "She's nowhere to be seen."

David looked at his watch. It was coming close to a quarter past nine. "When you say I'm devoid of any meaning, what exactly do you mean, Agent Carter?"

"Well, you have no clue who you are!" Carter proclaimed again.

"What does that mean?"

"You go from the factory to your house and from your house to the factory, isn't that right? You melt plastic, your only solution to your miserable life is Sarah, and here we are now in the car that the government is going to take away from you because of your negligence, looking for her, and she is nowhere to be found."

"How do you know she's nowhere to be found? Maybe she's at a friend's house!"

"Like I told you earlier, Davie boy, don't worry about Sarah."

"What's that supposed to mean again?"

"I'm sorry?"

"What does that mean? Don't worry about Sarah?"

"All I'm saying is your anxiety levels are too high. Just relax, will you?"

"Right. Well, I'll just repeat what I said earlier – you're only sticking around until she gets back."

"Let's go back to your humble abode, David. We aren't through yet."

"Through with what?"

"I told you, I want to know more about you. The more the merrier! You're the star of the show!"

Suspicion started to bubble to the surface of David's mind. Why was Carter so persistent? Was he trying to sniff around for a crime David had committed, something David wasn't aware of? Maybe he had done something without knowing, maybe he had dissociated one day and done something wrong. But he knew one thing for sure: he didn't like Carter. He didn't like the way he talked. Alarm bells were ringing through his mind, no matter how Carter tried to relax him and pull the wool over his eyes. He was starting to think that Carter was a threat. Why did he keep saying "Don't worry about Sarah" as if there was something he knew?

David had to make sure to take charge of the conversation from now on. He wouldn't dance for Carter anymore. "Alright, Agent Carter, as you wish."

"I like the determination in your voice, David. It's…exciting."

"Whatever."

"Yeah, I'll tell you whatever. Say bye-bye to your Ford Tempo, my friend."

David yanked the handbrake up and the tires screeched to a stop outside his house. "Do you really have to come back inside?" he asked, feeling more or less defeated by this persistent, irritating rash of a man.

"Tell me more about yourself, my friend. Tell me about your childhood."

"Why do you need to know about my childhood?" Now David was really starting to doubt his sanity. What if his suspicions were right? What if this Agent Carter was only fronting as a tax man? What if, throughout David's sad little life, he had developed a mental illness where he would commit crimes without noticing, leaving only blanks in his memory? What if Carter kept saying "Don't worry about Sarah" because in one of these memory lapses, David had unknowingly killed her?

He grabbed Agent Carter by his suit and pushed him up against the door. He squeezed his hand around his throat. "Where the hell is Sarah?"

Carter started to laugh maniacally. "How the hell am I supposed to know where she is?"

"You keep talking about her like there's something I don't know. Now, I don't know who the hell you are, who sent you or why you're so persistent about being around me, but you better tell me, otherwise I'll beat your ass to a pulp."

"Oh, looking to catch a little jail time now, are we, on top of everything else? Beating a government agent." He laughed. "Come on, David, you're smarter than that."

Their eyes met. David knew Carter was probably right, but he didn't like it. "Well, why don't you spend the night in the guest bedroom, since you're so adamant about getting to know me? Hell, why don't you spend a whole week with me! Maybe we can go fishing, too!"

"Oh no, David, that won't be necessary. A few more hours with you, that's all I want. And then everything – I mean, *I* shall be gone like the wind."

David stared him down hard and then unlocked the front door. Carter strolled in as if he owned the place and sat down on the couch across from where David was supposed to sit. He beckoned David over.

"You're a universe revolving around a universe, David!" said Carter, his manic enthusiasm returning.

"What in the hell is that supposed to mean?"

"There's just so much to explore about you that hasn't been explored! You're like a diamond mine – you can't expect me to start digging and then stop before I hit paydirt. Please, David. Go easy on me, pal."

David slumped down on the living room couch and covered his face with his hand. "Jesus Christ, are you insane? I thought you came here to tell me about my taxes!"

And then David's poor, paranoid little mind started to flirt with paranoid little thoughts. There was something he didn't know; he was doubting his own sanity. He was even starting to think that Agent Carter might not be real.

"Just tell me what the hell it is you want to know about me!" David finally burst out.

Agent Carter locked his gaze. "Alright, David, let's start with your childhood. Tell me about your childhood. Normal? Abnormal? Messed up?"

Who the hell is this guy anyway? thought David. *Tax man my ass! He must be a fed. I must have done something.*

"Now, don't be shy, David. Tell me as if you're telling an old friend. Isn't that what we are anyway? Old friends?"

Jesus Christ, he thought. *Now he's saying we're old friends. Should I call 911? Am I having a mental breakdown?*

"Don't start freaking out now, Davie boy. I can see you squirming around there. Just take everything I say with a pinch of salt."

"You really are a son of a bitch, do you know that, Agent Carter?"

"Getting defensive already! That's a good start, I like the way we're headed – my messed-up-childhood senses are tingling!"

"One more word comes out of your mouth and I'll beat your ass!" said David, ready to explode.

"Was that something your father may or may not have said to your mother when he came home drunk?"

"Excuse me?"

"You heard me. Sometimes when we're under examination or if we're put in a tight spot, we start going backward, regressing. Did you just regress into your childhood there for a moment?"

"I'm sorry, is this a goddamn psy-op or something? Are you really a tax man? Are you sure you're not a fed? Because if I've done something wrong, you can just tell me up-front. We don't need to go into this psychoanalysis bullcrap."

"Oh, but I think we do, David. And this isn't 'psychoanalysis bullcrap,' by the way. Just imagine you're talking to an old pal. Like me!"

"But you aren't my old friend! You're just some guy – some guy who came here to tell me they were going to take my car away – and now you've got me pinned down asking me awkward personal questions. I mean, what the hell is wrong with you, man?"

"Was your father a drunk?"

David felt like he was about to stand up and smash every piece of furniture in the room. "Yes! Yes, god damn it, he was a drunk! And he beat my mother! And he left us when I was five – Jesus Christ, what do you want from me?"

"Twelve thousand dollars overdue…" mumbled Carter.

"Twelve thousand dollars overdue?" repeated David. "So, I'm twelve thousand dollars overdue because of some insignificant thing that happened to me in my childhood?"

"Tsk, tsk, tsk. Come now, David. Insignificant? Think about it like a domino effect. It all adds up – all the numbers add up at the end of the day, David. I know that better than anyone. Wouldn't you say so, too?"

David was on the verge of tears. "Stop it. Just stop. Tell me what it is you want. Do you want me to slide a little envelope with some money in it under the table so you can go away? Because I can do that."

"No, no, no. David, stop fantasizing about the wrong things. This has nothing to do with money."

"This has everything to do with money! You're a tax collector!"

"No, David, this is about you, buddy. This is about the truth about you."

The truth? Maybe he is a fed. David's mind was racing faster than it ever had before. *Jesus Christ, I must have gone blank and killed Sarah!*

"What's going through your mind, Davie boy? I can see you are struggling."

"Did – did I kill Sarah?"

"Oh, now we really have hit paydirt – I've just found one of the biggest diamonds in the entire mine! But no, David, rest assured – and hey, when I tell you this, I'm giving you my word – rest assured, Sarah is safe. Or maybe she isn't, I don't know, because I don't know anything about you and Sarah. Why don't you go into that a little bit? And rest assured when I tell you, I – uh – the tax man, am a man of my word…Don't be a fool and believe me."

"Me and Sarah have been married for twenty years, god damn it! Why would I do anything to her?"

"When and where did you meet her?"

"We met when I was twenty. Back in seventy-six when I just got into college."

"Was it a romantic relationship? Passionate? Love at first sight, crazy romance story teetering on the edge of destruction, or were you guys a fairly reserved and decent couple?"

"We were decent," he said, as tears welled in his eyes again. "Jesus Christ, where is she?"

"I told you not to worry about that."

"But you keep saying that over and over like there's something that you know."

"Alright, let's change the subject, I don't want you to keep worrying. Tell me about your teenage years. Must have been the early seventies, am I right?"

"Yeah."

"Hippies everywhere. Were you a naughty boy who went for the fruit of life, the tree of knowledge?"

"What?"

"I'm talking about acid, dumbass. Did you ever do acid? Ever try a little around a campfire singing kumbaya?"

"I don't need to say a word about that."

"I'm not a policeman, David. I'm your friend the tax collector. You can tell me if you did one little naughty thing once in your lifetime at a time when everyone else was doing it anyway!"

"Alright. I tried a quarter of a tab. Arrest me and let's get this over with."

Carter burst out into hysterical laughter. "Arrest me and let's get this over with, he says! Oh man, you're hilarious. What did it feel like?"

"More or less what you would imagine it feels like, dancing around with the pixies and the fairies."

"So, you fried your brain good, huh? Pulled a Syd Barrett?"

And once again, David found himself flirting with those little paranoid thoughts. *I fried my brain, that's why I ended up working in a factory. They fired me from my actual job because they thought I was crazy!*

The truth about David is that he was always a sensitive man; he couldn't handle a government job like the one he ended up in after college. Everyone there had picked on him because he was vulnerable, so he quit and went to live a more low-key life. Heck, he was even doing good for the environment, working in recycling.

David started talking to himself: "He knows he's an asshole, he knows he is one. No, I did not 'fry my brain,' you cretin. I only ever did it once and that was it."

"Hippies," said Carter. "There are tons of them I visit, even to this day. The real old-school ones. They never pay taxes either. What do you think of them now? The hippies, I mean."

"Losers."

"Exactly, David. Losers. Losers who have assets seized, losers who are still playing guitar on the streets. Are you a loser, David, or are you a winner?"

"I'm neither."

"You see, this is why we're taking away your Ford Tempo. Because you can't admit to yourself that you won. You see, I work in the government, David. And before I came here, I did a little bit of digging. I know they gave you hell. You're not a loser, pal, you're just sensitive. Lighten up on me a little bit will you, jeez."

David sighed a tremendous sigh. He'd almost forgotten about Sarah as he wove in and out of Carter's web, but the thought of her came back to him. "It's ten o'clock at night. She never stays out this late. That's it – I'm calling the police and declaring her missing."

"Oh, you don't have to do that."

"Stop yapping at me. You're just some idiot who knows nothing at all and thinks it's funny to badger me until I go insane. I'm calling the police."

"Alright. Go ahead. But first, let me tell you that a senior of mine – we call him Johnny Rocket – said we should try squeezing fifteen grand out of you and that me and him could split the remaining three. I came here with the truth. And rest assured, I know, somewhere deep down in my heart, that Sarah is just fine."

"Shut up."

"Okay, have it your way."

"You know what, I'll just call her on her cell phone first, and if she doesn't pick up, I'll call the police."

"An excellent idea!"

David had a flip phone and so did Sarah. When he got it out, Carter remarked, "So that's where the money you're supposed to be paying your taxes and bringing children into this world with is going. Flip phones, huh?"

"Sarah and I don't spend a lot of time together," said David. "Sometimes I like to call her when I'm on my break at the factory." He dialed her number. Three loud beeps then straight to voicemail. "Her battery is dead..." he said with cloudy eyes. "That's it, I'm calling the police."

"Call the police!"

David dialed 911 and told them his wife had gone missing. They asked for a description of her appearance.

"Shoulder-length, chestnut-brown hair. Green eyes. Freckles. She was wearing jeans and a green sweater."

After that, there was nothing he could do but wait.

"Do you think they'll find her?" asked Carter with a menacing little hint of irony.

David slumped back on the couch and covered his eyes. He didn't say a word. He could feel Carter watching him, and his mind raced with paranoid thoughts to fill the eerie silence. He had no clue what was going on. He didn't know if Carter was a fed, if this was all just a test of sanity for him and he had killed her after going blank, or if in five minutes she would be home and then everything would be over.

Carter sighed, feeling bored. David was cooked. But surely there was something further he could talk to him about. "Have you ever heard of multiple personality disorder?" he asked with a little half-smile cut across his face.

David started panicking again. "I have."

"Did you know that there was an operation in the sixties called Project MK-Ultra, where the government literally induced multiple personality disorder in people through some really messed-up psychological testing methods?"

"I can't say I've ever heard of Project MK-Ultra, no."

"Hmm…So you don't know much about these sorts of things then, do you?"

David erupted. "I never cared about this psychobabble bullcrap, no! All I care about is my job and my wife for the time being, is that a problem?"

"Can I take a look around your house?"

This was the moment, David figured, that Agent Carter would discover Sarah's body and reveal to David that he had multiple personality disorder and had killed her after switching to a different personality. Carter had truly done a number on the poor man since entering his home.

"Just…do what you're here for," said David.

"What am I here for?" asked Carter, throwing David off balance again.

His shoulders slumped downward, defeated. "I barely know anymore."

"Well, lighten up on me, pal – all I want to do is look around the house! I really like looking at the stuff people hang on their walls – paintings, pictures, ornaments. Doesn't that excite you, too?"

Carter took to the staircase where all the framed pictures were hung. He stopped instantly when he found their wedding picture. "Well, look here!" he said, triumphant as usual. He took the picture to David. "She's a very pretty young lady."

"Please…don't…talk about my wife."

"What about you, Davie boy? What's with you in this picture? I mean, look at the way you're looking at the camera. It's just a weird stare, man, isn't it? Glossed-over, glassy eyes. You don't seem as happy as she is in this picture."

"What's that supposed to mean?"

"Can I keep looking around?"

David scrunched up his eyes and rubbed them with his fingers. "You can keep looking around."

"What time did she leave the house?" said Carter, scanning over the other pictures and paintings.

"I don't know, I was at work."

"She didn't call you? Tell you where she was going?"

"She's a grown woman, she can go wherever she wants."

"You guys happy together, or is it a monotone life? You wake up, go to work, she does the housework, you come home, she makes you a microwave dinner, you two stare blankly at the TV and go to bed, or is there still a flare of life in any of this?"

Carter was like a berating voice stuck in his head. "Why do you want to know what our marriage is like?"

"Well, she hasn't come home at the usual time, as you said yourself. What if she's seeing someone else? What if she has been seeing someone else for a while now? Tired of the stale existence you provide her with?"

Now pieces of the puzzle seemed to fit. Sarah could have been having an affair, and David might have found out about it, committed a crime of passion and was now living in denial about ever doing so.

"So, you're saying she's been having an affair?" asked David, now thinking of Carter as some kind of all-knowing entity.

"Well, it's a possibility, right? I mean, I've been divorced twice for the very same reason. Except I was the one doing the cheating." He laughed.

"You're a real piece of work, you know that?"

"Are you a violent man, David? Do you have violent thoughts? Do you enjoy violence on TV?"

David started doubting himself again. For the most part, he was a man of simple tastes, but maybe there was a part of him that did enjoy violence.

"I don't know."

"You don't know?"

"No. I said I don't know."

"Well, what *do* you know?" asked Carter, puncturing deeper and deeper with every question.

"Agent Carter, what's the point of all this? I mean, do you know something I don't? Have I done something wrong that I can't remember doing? Did I do something to Sarah?"

"Twelve thousand dollars overdue," Carter repeated. His eyes were bloodshot, David noticed.

"You're not answering my question."

"I ask the questions here."

Sarah had officially been declared a missing person. David had given up, given in to Carter. He was at his mercy now.

"You're one of the most messed-up people I've ever met," said Carter, his tone growing grave.

"How's that?"

"You don't even trust your own judgment anymore, do you? Did you kill Sarah, David?"

"I'm begging you, Agent Carter, please just tell me what's going on. Please just tell me if I did."

"I told you not to worry about Sarah."

"Then why the hell are you asking me if I've killed her?"

"Do you know how detectives interrogate suspects?"

"So, these are all mind games. You're looking for a confession, is that right? You just want to hear it coming out of my mouth. You're not really a tax man, are you? Are you wearing a wire right now?"

"Tell me, David, are you sane or insane?"

"I don't know anymore."

"You don't know? Well, what do you—"

David slammed his fist on the coffee table. "I'll gouge your eyes out, you bastard!"

"So, you are a violent man."

David couldn't tell up from down, left from right. He was starting to breathe heavily, entering a full-blown panic attack. "Please!" he begged. "I can't breathe!" The room was spinning as he rapidly gulped down air. He slouched forward, gripping his chest firmly. The waves of anxiety forced him to the floor, where he curled up, knees tucked into his chest, and heaved for air.

"Come here, buddy," said Carter, who knelt on the floor to cradle him. "Just breathe, everything's going to be alright. I promise. I won't badger you anymore, I promise. Here, take down my number. If Sarah doesn't get home by eleven tomorrow morning, give me a call. I'll be back to offer you as much help as I can. Oh, and I should be back around that time anyway so we can seize your car, so whether you call me or not, I'll be here."

"Okay, okay…" said David, trying to hold on.

"Okay." Carter started stroking his hair. "Relax, buddy, shhh…Don't worry about a thing. Your old friend Agent Carter has you covered."

Pushing David away from him, Carter got up from the floor and dusted himself off. He picked up his briefcase and left. The front door shut behind him.

David burst into tears. He had no clue what he had just gone through and he needed Sarah desperately. But she was nowhere to be found.

David stayed awake until three in the morning until he mechanically shut down, trying to process everything in the void of sleep. And even then, it was extremely difficult. He was cornered into an empty space, where all that existed was nothingness.

CHAPTER 2

Sure enough, Carter was back in the morning with a few government goons, who took the keys to David's Ford Tempo, sputtered it up into gear and drove off with it.

"You see, that's what happens when you're twelve thousand dollars overdue, my friend," said Carter lightheartedly as he patted David on the shoulder, looking at him in the morning light.

"I don't give a damn about the car. Where's Sarah?"

"We'll get into that in a minute, as soon as you invite me in for a cup of coffee."

"Oh no, you aren't going to fool me this time, Carter. Either you tell me where she is now, or I carry on looking for her on my own."

"First off, it's Agent Carter. Remember when I told you that? Secondly, I've done some digging around myself, so you might as well invite me into your home." His tone softened, giving the impression there was something he knew that could be useful to David.

David laughed in disbelief. "Digging around?"

"Yes."

"Alright, *Agent* Carter. Come in."

They sat down facing each other with the coffee table between them.

"So, Agent Carter. You said you have some information about my wife's whereabouts?" David started off the conversation more collected than he'd anticipated he would be.

"Papa Greg," said Carter, taking a sip of his coffee and nearly choking on it. He coughed out the words again. "Papa Greg."

"What?"

"You mean to tell me you don't know who Papa Greg is?"

"Hell no, I don't know who 'Papa Greg' is."

"Real American hero," said Carter, his voice oddly perky. "Everybody knows Papa Greg. He lives in your area. He sits on the porch all day long with his double-barrel, checking out the neighborhood for trouble. He keeps an eye out for anything bad that might happen in the area, which makes him your man. I approached Papa Greg last night after you had your little panic attack, offered him five dollars, and I asked him if he'd seen Sarah, and gave him the same description you gave the cops. Do you know what he said to me?"

"Has he seen her?" asked David, pulse rising.

"No, he just stroked his mustache, and all he said to me was the only thing he gives a damn about is his hair, his ciggies and his coffee. He also added it was a shame you hadn't been paying your taxes because, despite the Tempo's reputation, he thinks it's a nice car."

"That's what you came inside to tell me? That's what your so-called 'digging around' for information about my missing wife was?"

"Yep."

"Oh, Jesus Christ…" said David, putting his hand on his forehead and massaging it to get rid of the tension.

"Now, what have I told you over and over again, David? Don't worry about Sarah. Uh, let's just say Agent Carter here has been on this case for a very long time, made some predictions, taken charge of the situation. Sarah, she'll be just fine."

"God damn it, what the hell do you mean by that?"

"That's none of your concern right now. That'll be my concern."

"She's *my* wife!"

"What's your relationship been like for the past year? I'm guessing pretty stagnant, right?"

"Excuse me? What are you implying?"

"Nothing. I'm just asking questions."

"Look. You've taken my car. You've gotten what you wanted out of me '*officially*,' am I correct? What business is it of yours to be asking those types of questions? Why do you keep telling me not to worry about Sarah? Are you hiding something from me, Agent Carter? Because I'll tell you what, your little interrogation thing you've got going, your little drill here, it's freaking me out."

Carter took a long, drawn-out sip of his coffee and stared at the ceiling a little while, then he blinked a couple of times and, after a gasp of relief, turned his attention back toward David. "Stagnant relationship, David? Yes or no?"

"God damn you. Yes! Alright! Yes! Our relationship has been stagnant! But isn't that normal for any couple that's been married for twenty years? They go out for meals and don't talk to each other, they focus more on house chores rather than each other. I mean, for god's sake, you said you've had several divorces, Agent Carter, don't you know what marriage is like?"

"So, she's been asking for children?"

"Several times, yes."

"And you can't give her any because you don't have what it takes to provide, you sorry, impotent, stupid son of a bitch."

David couldn't believe what had just come out of this guy's mouth. The sheer audacity behind his words, the drilling, the questioning. "You got some nerve, you know that, Agent Carter?"

"Look, David. This is like a jigsaw puzzle with the pieces scattered around everywhere on the floor. We gotta do the math here, you and me, together – we're in this together – so if I ever hurt your pride, just know I'm doing it for your own good."

"Okay, but what are you actually implying here?"

"Listen, David – uh, when women aren't, uh, properly *taken care of*," he said, lowering his voice to a whisper, "they get disappointed. And when they get disappointed, that's when they go looking around for other relations."

"So, you think she's been cheating on me?"

"It's a possibility. Dreams sometimes do come true."

"What?"

"Dreams."

"Dreams?"

"Do you dream some crazy shit at night?" Carter asked David with a genuine interest.

David's pulse started rising. Carter was going into shrink-interrogator mode again. Psy-op fed mode.

"Agent Carter, I'm a forty-year-old man. I don't get much sleep and when I do it's usually just a blank."

"A blank, huh?"

"Yeah, a blank."

"See, I get these dreams where I'm trying to solve something that can't be solved," said Carter, and David got the weird sensation that something had just been solved in Carter's mind.

"This 'going blank' business of mine…"

"Sarah's fine."

David was on the verge of tears again. "What do you *want* from me, Agent Carter?"

"She's still missing, but she's fine."

"Agent Carter…what do you want?"

"What's your opinion of me, David?"

"I can't tell…You're a maverick…a jack of all trades – you seem to know so much, but damn it do you reveal so very little."

"I'll take the maverick thing as a compliment then?"

"You can if you want to."

"Thank you for the compliment. But the truth is, David – uh – I'm a lonely guy. And you're an old friend in a predicament—"

"Old friend? We've started with the old friend thing again?"

"There's just something about you that makes me feel like I've known you for a very long time."

"How'd you figure that one?"

"Because you're an open book to me. You don't even have to talk and I can read your goddamn mind. You don't have to talk and it's like you've been talking to me for an hour and a half!"

David was starting to think he was becoming part of a covert government experiment, something like that MK-Ultra bullcrap Carter had been talking about.

"Where's Sarah?" he found the courage to ask.

"I don't know, but I am one hundred per cent certain that she's alright."

"How can you know that if you don't know where she is?"

"That's something you're just going to have to wait to find out."

"So, you do know something?"

"I know nothing about her whereabouts. I'm just telling you. If you think I know more than you, you might be right or – uh – you might be wrong. Ambiguity is of the essence when subjects like yourself come around. And you're the specimen of the century."

"You don't scare me, agent. You don't have any power over me."

"There you go again, getting defensive, getting paranoid. What are you gaining out of this?"

"Where's Sarah?"

"She's fine."

"Where is she?"

"Paranoid, paranoid little man."

"So now you're coming up with another defect in me? I know I get paranoid, you don't need to tell me that."

"Dreams, David. Dreams. Are you sane or insane? I can't figure that out for you."

"And how is an insane man meant to figure out he's insane?"

"What about sane men – how do they know they're sane, then? See, life is like walking a tightrope. You have to keep balancing. Sometimes things we carry with us, things from our past or even fears about the future, make us lose balance."

"Are you referring to me when you say that?"

"Yes."

"Why?"

"Twelve thousand dollars overdue."

"Okay, twelve thousand dollars overdue – I couldn't give a crap if it was a million! Why are you saying I'm insane? Why are you making me doubt myself?"

"You aren't doubting anything. You're getting closer to the truth."

"So, I'm nuts now, right?"

"I don't know – are you?"

David gave it a little thought. And then a smile appeared on his face. Then, sure this whole conversation was being recorded by a wire Carter was wearing under his shirt, he burst out laughing like a maniac.

"I'm crazy..." David started singing. "Crazy for feeling so lonely!"

There was a look of pure satisfaction on Carter's face. He had managed to break him down. He went in for the kill. "David, do you ever get the funny feeling that it's not just your own voice in your head? That there could be other voices?"

"Don't cry for me...Argentina!" David continued singing.

Carter was holding on very tightly to prevent himself from bursting out in triumphant laughter. "Ah, settle down, settle down, David."

"Settle down, settle down!" David mocked.

"Answer the goddamn question."

"Agent Carter, if I was insane, would I be able to hold a job down at a factory, or would these little voices in my head tell me to jump into the furnace where we melt the plastic?"

"Okay, so, you don't hear voices?"

"No."

"So, you're sane?"

David thought again about the wire underneath Carter's shirt. If he admitted he was sane and he had done something to Sarah without meaning to in one of these blank time lapses, he could go in for life.

"Sane?"

"Are you a sane man, David?"

"Sanity is a mysterious thing, Agent Carter, it comes and it goes."

"So, you aren't sane?"

David was cornered. What if they took him to a madhouse? "Can we change the discussion?" he asked, somewhat desperately.

Agent Carter smiled. "Sure, yeah, yeah. Sure."

Relief washed over David.

"So back to Sarah," said Carter, knowing that every word he said made David more uncertain, "I tried my best. If Papa Greg doesn't know where she is then she could be anywhere, right?"

"Is Papa Greg some kind of security camera? How the hell is he meant to know where my wife is?"

"Papa Greg knows everything," said Carter. "He's a war veteran, served twice in Vietnam. He trudged through the mud in the jungles at night with eyes as wide as an owl's, looking for the Vietcong."

"And what does that have to do with him knowing where Sarah is?"

"Well, have you asked anyone else? Any of the neighbors, any of her relatives?"

"That's probably the smartest thing you've asked since her disappearing," said David.

"Well, I am a man of reason, David. I pay my taxes."

"How does me paying my taxes have anything to do with Sarah and the neighbors or her relatives? See, there you go again, flipping things round!"

"Call her parents."

"What?"

"I said, call her parents. If they don't know where she is then this is going to turn into a little murder mystery kinda thing – and as much as you think I want that, you're wrong," said Carter.

"Alright, alright. I'll call her parents."

David flipped open his phone and dialed his father-in-law's cell. It took about twenty-six seconds for him to pick up. The harshest twenty-six seconds of David's life.

"Hey, Chris," said David to his father-in-law. "Can you hear me?"

Carter could only faintly hear Chris's voice on the other end of the line.

"Why am I calling?" David asked Chris. "It's about Sarah."

"Give me the phone," said Carter.

"Wait just a sec, Chris – what?"

"Give me the phone."

"Why?"

"Just give it to me."

David reluctantly handed the phone over to Carter, still stunned by his audacity.

"Hey, Chris!" said Carter, in a jolly yet authoritative voice. "Yeah, this is Agent Carter. Your son-in-law has just had his car seized. Listen, have you, uh, by any chance heard from Sarah these past couple of days?"

All David could hear from Chris was a faint murmuring; he couldn't actually make out any of the words.

"Mhmm, mhmm," went Carter. "Yeah…Yeah. Mhmm, and when did that happen? Okay. Okay. Alright, Chris, it's been lovely talking to you, yeah. Yeah, me and your son-in-law go way back, no need to worry – been good pals for a real long time. Bye now."

Carter closed the cell phone and handed it back to David, who was shocked and on full alert.

"W-what did he say?"

"Yeah, according to Chris he hasn't heard much from Sarah yesterday or today, but a few days before yesterday she called him and told you you were acting funny – in his own words, you were being a bit of a *'freak.'* According to her, of course."

"Wait, what?"

"You heard me. A *freak.*"

"She said that about me?"

Pretending that this saddened him, Carter looked to the floor and simply said, "Yes…yes."

"When you say freak, what do you mean? Like a psycho freak, or what?"

"She's fine, for Christ's sake! Haven't I told you that a million times?"

David was still worried he had gone into one of those blank-outs, maybe killed her. That had been his theory for a while now, but every time he tried to ask about it, Carter had shut him down.

"Listen, Agent Carter." He gulped, collecting himself. "You don't need to go easy on me. If I've done something to her, just come right out and say it."

"You think – or rather, you're genuinely convinced – you may have done something to Sarah?"

"Y-yes." There was a tremor in David's voice.

"I told you that you were a diamond mine," said Carter in awe.

CHAPTER 3

"Listen – uh – David…Like I said quite a few times, I'm just the tax man here, but I want you to know that I feel like me and you, uh, we've been friends for a while now, haven't we?"

"Yeah," said David, taking the bait. "Yeah – we've been friends for a while."

Those little paranoid thoughts he flirted with came and went, came and went, and in this moment, when Carter had caught him off guard, he wasn't in the paranoid state of mind. For now.

"So, what do you say we try and unravel this little mystery here as a team? You know, you cooperate and we come to some kind of a conclusion." Carter's eyes twinkled in delight.

Now David became paranoid again. It was the word "cooperate" that did it.

"Can I ask you something?" said David, tensely.

"Shoot."

"Are you really a tax man or are you some kind of a federal agent?"

Carter burst out in hysterical laughter. He couldn't help himself. But at the same time, he also realized he'd been handed another card to play.

"David, David, David. For a factory worker who spends the whole day melting plastic, you sure have got some wild imagination. Or maybe it's not your imagination at all – maybe, uh, it's like you got this sixth sense kinda thing going on here."

"What's that supposed to mean?"

"Twelve thousand dollars overdue and he still doesn't get it."

"Right, twelve thousand dollars overdue, *and*?"

"And what?"

"You never answered my question."

"What question?"

"Are you a federal agent?"

Carter stared at him wildly. With a tremendous force of rage behind his eyes, he slammed his hand on the coffee table and said, "I ask the questions here!"

And from that point on…well…let's just say those suspicions failed to leave the back of David's mind.

Carter breathed heavily, calming himself down. He couldn't allow high-intensity moments like that to throw things off track. "I'm sorry," he said. "Didn't mean to lose it like that."

"That's alright." David was still confused.

Their eyes met briefly. David was, he realized, sitting opposite what was probably one of the most peculiar men he had met in his entire life.

"Well, go on!" urged Carter.

"Go on, what?"

"Say something! We gotta solve this mystery – this is your wife we're talking about here."

"Right. Right. She said I was acting like a freak. That doesn't sound too much like her."

"Do you think I just made that up?" asked Carter, staring him down.

"That's not what I'm saying, no."

"Well, thank god for that. God forbid you think your old pal Agent Carter is making things up now."

"Well, if she said that then maybe there's something I don't know."

"What was Sarah like, as a person?" asked Carter with a mixture of enthusiasm and curiosity.

"She was the bubbly type for quite a long time, always out with a friend or always engaging in some kind of recreational activity, like going for walks in nature. It's just…these past couple of years, job's been tough, living's been tight, wages have gone down and all, so she stopped seeing things so brightly."

"Oh, I see. So, it's your impotence again, isn't it?"

"Why do you always have to criticize me?"

"Well, maybe Sarah's been criticizing you. That's more important than me criticizing you, surely?"

"You think her life's gotten worse because of me?"

"Listen, I used to know this guy – we seized a couple of his assets also. He was a priest living in a shitty little neighborhood surrounded by nothing, and he had this wife, right? And one night, she just ran away. She couldn't take him anymore, she had the overwhelming impulse to escape."

"Is that why you keep saying she's fine? Is it because she's just left me and you somehow happen to know that?"

"No, it was an example, that's all. No, David – I think there's something weirder going on here."

"Weirder, like what?"

"I'll be honest with you, Davie boy, I'm a weird guy myself. Whenever I tell you she's fine, do you know what my thinking is behind that?"

"No."

"Well, I'm something of a troubled soul myself – uh – and basically, let's just put it this way, sometimes I believe people are better off being dead than alive. Like they're in a better place or something, do you understand?"

"Oh no…" Tears pricked at David's eyes. "Sarah, no…"

"Oh, stop crying like a little girl. No one told you she's dead. I'm just explaining my rationale."

"So, is she alive or is she dead?" he said, wiping a tear from his eyes.

"How am I supposed to know? You tell me, David."

"But you know everything," said David. "Please tell me you know everything!"

"I know enough."

"So, she's dead, isn't she? And this is just a long, drawn-out interrogation, isn't it? *I don't know if it was me or if it was someone else!* Just tell me and be gone!"

"When you say someone else…what do you mean exactly?"

"Exactly what it sounds like. Someone else."

"Have you ever thought there could be someone else living in you?"

That threw him off. Now David had a new predicament, a direct threat, a direct question. Sane, or insane? He remained silent, in deep contemplation.

"What do you think?" he finally asked Carter, genuinely concerned.

"Oh relax, David. We all have other selves – I'm not the same agent when I'm seizing cars and I'm not the same agent when I've stopped somewhere for a coffee. We – uh – exist in different modalities, do you see?"

"So…I'm…not…crazy, then?"

"Let's say you had murdered Sarah. I couldn't decide that in a court of law. That would be up to the psychiatrists."

"*But you're here collecting evidence. Aren't you?*"

"Look, I'm a tax agent, not a federal one."

"And how can I be sure of that?"

"I give you my word."

"You told me not to trust your word."

"Well, you see, sometimes life can get trippy, can't it?"

Tense with pent-up frustration, David fell into a defeated mood. He was just a tool to be manipulated by Carter. He wasn't the sort of man to strike another man, fight back or defend himself, and Carter got off on that.

David started pacing up and down the room. He opened his flip phone again and tried dialing Sarah – three beeps, then straight to voicemail.

"God damn it," he said, fiercely wound up and wounded.

"The ball's always been in your court," said Carter. "Just like it was with your taxes. Oh, David, surely you must already know where she is. Deep down in your heart, you must know."

"She's – she's dead. Or she's with another man. Or I caught her with another man, then killed her. Agent Carter, please, I can't take this anymore."

"One minute," said Carter. "You can't tell the difference between reality and fantasy right now, can you?"

David was being wound tighter and tighter. "I don't know. Damn it, Agent Carter, please."

"How do you know if I'm real?"

"Because I can hear you, I can touch you – I know you're real."

"That doesn't mean a goddamn thing – you could be hallucinating. Old Agent Carter could just be a figment of your imagination. Or maybe Agent Carter is the other you. Maybe Agent Carter is your alter ego, the one who killed Sarah."

David was reduced to tears again. He balled up his fist and bit his knuckles, eyes cloudy, judgment totally destroyed.

"So, you're me and I'm you?" he said, choking on his words.

Carter started giggling like a fool.

"And now you're – you're laughing?" David couldn't believe it.

"I have just found one of the rarest gems I have ever come across," said Carter with pure delight, continuing to giggle.

David stood there across from him, his eyes streaming with tears, and just looked at him. It was the strangest sensation to know that the man he was facing could be the worst thing that had ever happened to him in his life.

"Twelve thousand dollars overdue," said Carter, dead serious now.

"Yeah. Yeah, I know, you're right. You keep saying that so you must be right. Twelve thousand dollars overdue, this is all my fault. There must be a deeper meaning when you say that, too, because you *keep saying it*. This is all my fault. Agent Carter?"

"Yes, my boy?"

"Could you get me checked-in to the nearest psych ward?"

"Ah, come on now, that's not necessary."

"But I'm losing my mind."

"Oh, come on, David. First off, stop pacing around the room and sit down. Second, take a hold of yourself, man! Get a grip on the situation! She's not here! Okay? What does that mean? Do we go insane, or do we do what a real man would do and solve the puzzle?"

David squeaked like a blind little mouse and bit on his balled-up fist again. He was distraught, hysterical. "I don't know!" he cried. "I don't know what to do!"

"I'll point you in the right direction. Maybe you didn't murder her. Maybe she's done something to herself? I mean, you said you've had a miserable couple of years, right? Maybe she's just wandered off into the woods like a stray cat on the verge of death."

David exhaled loudly. The guilt started to simmer down a little. If it wasn't him, and she had decided to do something to herself, then maybe – no. It still nagged at his very core. There was no relief.

"Yeah, but two minutes ago you said that I'm you and you're me, and one of us killed her…Now you're saying it's a suicide? So, does that make you real? Does that make me real? This situation – it's just too much. I can't trust a word you say anymore."

"But you have to trust me!" yelled Carter. "We're in this together! This is you and me. I'm the one who came knocking yesterday and I'm the one who stuck it out with you. And I made a vow to myself, I'm not leaving you until we find Sarah."

"So – you are real?"

"I'm real. But what is real, David? Do either of us even know anymore? Hell, I'm starting to lose my marbles, too!"

"So, you don't know a goddamn thing either, do you, Agent Carter?" said David, who started to collect himself. "All you're here to do is mess with my friggin' head!"

"I never said anything of the sort."

"So, where is she?"

"Look, I'm not psychic – I can't close my eyes and draw you a map of where she is like they did in Project Stargate, but there's one thing I do know, David, and that's that she's fine where she is."

"Well, that could mean she's dead, according to what you said earlier! And what in the hell is Project Stargate?"

"Haven't you heard about it? It was declassified last year. Psychic spies in the government. Cool stuff, if you ask me."

"First it's Project MK-Ultra, now it's Project Stargate – well, what in the hell project do you call this then? Project Let's Drive David Insane?"

"I'm sorry, David, let me just get this straight. Do you think it's me that's torturing you, or is it every tick of the clock on the wall? Every second you have no awareness of her whereabouts, no certainty about whether your cognitive abilities have some-how been impaired?"

The conversation was getting nauseating. There were too many loose ends. Too many possibilities to think about. David finally sat down again, opposite the man that had barged in and taken control of basically every facet of his life, unin-vited, unaccounted for. But he was making a serious impact. And David couldn't control that. His simplemindedness was his weakness, his skin wasn't thick enough, and he couldn't see through the fog and figure out what was going on with that Agent Carter: whether he was his alter ego, whether he was a federal agent, whether he was just a tax man looking to bully some poor middle-aged man.

"So, what do I do now?" asked David, his eyes drooping in defeat.

"Have you checked back with the police?"

"No – but...that's – that's a good idea."

David dialed 911 for the follow-up call. Tension was high, and he was catastrophizing even before they picked up. On the other end of the receiver, there was some fifty-year-old tub of lard. David could hear the fat jiggling in her gullet as she re-sponded to the call.

"Yes, it's David. I called about Sarah going missing last night, I don't know if you remember that?"

"Oh, we remember."

"Right – so – have you been looking? Have you managed to trace her anywhere?"

"Look, sir. We have some bad news. We found a body down by the lake near the woods."

"Oh god – no. Please no."

"It wasn't her."

"What do you mean?"

"We think there's a night prowler around killing innocent women because we've been getting quite a few more calls about missing women. I would sit tight and let us do our job, Mr. – Daniel, was it?"

"David."

"David, yeah. Sit tight, sir. I'm sure we'll find her."

She hung up before he had the chance to ask any other questions.

Carter was alert. "Well? What did they say?"

"There's a serial killer out there. They found a body by the lake, but it wasn't hers," replied David, a depleted shell of a man, but with relief that it wasn't Sarah's body.

"A serial killer?" said Carter, shocked, but with a hint of amusement on his face. "Really?"

David sighed miserably, sat back down and covered his eyes. "Was it us? Was it me and you? Agent Carter? My serial killer alter ego?"

"Oh, pull yourself together, man. How could I possibly be your alter ego? If I had to guess what an alter ego would look like for you it would probably be some idiotic government employee who takes himself seriously and thinks he's doing good for the world."

"So, you, then!"

"Me?"

"Isn't that what you do?"

"I do nothing of the sort. When the tax man knocks on your door, it's not about doing good for the world. How did you come to that conclusion? It's to make someone's life utterly miserable!"

"Well, you've done a damn good job at that."

"All I've done is try to help you. Well – aside from taking your car away and all that bureaucratic bullcrap."

"How? How have you tried to help me?"

"Well, haven't I been a comforting presence? Like someone you've known for a very long time, an old friend giving his buddy comfort, a shoulder to cry on type thing?"

David simply couldn't protect himself; he fell prey to that idea, too. "Yeah, you're like an old friend. You've been supportive enough – at times – I guess, so…maybe you're right."

"Well, there you go!" said Carter with a beaming grin, slapping David on the knee. "And let's not forget that one phrase I keep repeating…You're twelve thousand dollars overdue!"

David nodded. He was a little marionette, and Carter was pulling the strings. "Yeah, twelve thousand dollars overdue…"

CHAPTER 4

"You ever heard about a guy called Jeffrey Dahmer?" asked Carter. "Back in ninety-one they convicted him for being a serial killer."

"Yeah, I know about Dahmer."

"Did you also know he was a closet homosexual?" A little glint appeared in Carter's eyes.

"No, I didn't look into it that deeply. I was more concerned with happier things."

"Right, right. You know there's another word for happy, right?"

"What? Do you mean the word 'gay?' Yeah, but that's an old word. People don't use it that way anymore."

"Well, this way or that way, I gotta ask you a question, David, and please don't take this one too personally."

"Go on."

"Are you a closet homosexual?"

That was the one for David. His face turned red, there was a vein protruding from his neck and forehead and he slammed his hand on the coffee table. "How dare you!" he screamed. "I've been married nearly twenty goddamn years – longer than any of your marriages, pal – so don't you even go there!"

"Touchy, touchy, I wasn't expecting such an explosive reaction. Denial, they say – it, uh, brews anger."

David violently pointed his finger at Carter. "Don't you dare go there!"

"David, I never knew you had this side to you!"

"What goddamn side?" he said, bright red.

"This rage! It's intense!"

"Well, what do you expect, going and asking a question like that?"

"Alright, I'm sorry, we'll change the subject. Sarah, David. Did you ever have any violent outbursts with Sarah throughout your marriage? You told me that the past couple of years haven't been too great."

"Hmm, let me think," replied David sarcastically, "have I had any fights with Sarah? Of course we've had arguments. Tell me a couple that doesn't argue."

"Yeah, but, what kind of arguments? Were they this intense? Like the outburst you had just now?"

"I – I don't know. I don't know. Whenever I get this angry, I usually can't remember what comes next."

"Aha! And there you go."

"So, it was me who killed her? And maybe I killed the woman down by the lake. Who knows, maybe I've been on a spree!"

"Well, we can't confirm that, David, I'm afraid."

"Maybe you killed her – maybe I'm just hallucinating and talking to my alter ego, who is also in denial and confused about whether or not he killed his wife! You're me and I'm you, isn't that right, Carter?"

"*Agent* Carter. Please always remember to address me properly."

"*Agent* Carter. *Agent* Carter. Let me ask you something, pal, and this time I want a proper answer. Are you real, fake, a tax man or a federal agent?"

"What do you think?"

"I don't know what to believe."

"Well, there you go. If you can't trust yourself, how are you going to trust me? I'm a tax man."

David narrowed his eyes. "Let me see under your shirt."

"Woah there, pal, I thought you said you weren't into that kind of thing!"

"I wanna see if you're wearing a wire."

"Very well."

Agent Carter unbuttoned his shirt. All David could see was his chest.

"Lower," said David, with narrowed eyes.

"David!"

"Lower, damn it!"

Agent Carter exposed his belly to David, and sure enough, there was no wire.

"Doesn't mean a goddamn thing. You're probably still a fed," said David.

"See, I told you – you can't trust yourself."

"Is that me just talking to myself in the form of a tax man? Just tell me straight, even if you're a hallucination – did we kill that girl down by the lake?"

"I really couldn't tell you, David."

"Oh, stop acting innocent. It was us, wasn't it? Why don't I just turn myself in!"

"David, I really wouldn't do that, you know – I personally would never take credit for someone else's bad behavior."

"You just want us to survive! To keep on murdering innocent women!"

"David – really? How broken a man are you? Would you rather believe that you're some kind of insane lunatic who has killed his wife and another woman down by the lake over the plain and simple fact that she's just gone?"

"Gone? Gone where? Spit it out."

"Well, I hypothesize she's having an affair with some lawyer or doctor or something. The kind of guy that would be able to give her a family and wouldn't be *twelve thousand dollars* behind on taxes."

"Oh yeah?"

"Yeah!"

"And how can you be so certain of that, whoever you are, Mister Tax Man, Mister Alter Ego, Mister Federal Agent? Whoever the *hell* you are!"

"Hell. That's just it, isn't it? That's what you're going through right now."

"Damn straight it is."

"Hmm. Do you know what I would like?"

"What's that?"

"Well, it's about four-thirty in the afternoon – I've been here a while, pretending to be your, uh, therapist…I'd like a nice cup of coffee now, if that's alright with you, David. And while you're at it, have you got anything to nibble on? Like a biscuit or something?"

"I want you out of my goddamn house and out of my goddamn head, right now!"

"David...David, please simmer down and cooperate."

"You ever heard of the Second Amendment, pal? How about I go grab my double-barrel and put an end to this all?"

"What, by killing me, or yourself? You don't even know who's who!"

"Crap, damn it, friggin' go to hell!"

"Come on now, David – I guarantee you there is a pot of gold at the end of the rainbow that is called Agent Carter if you do cooperate."

"Cooperate, huh? Meaning?"

"Meaning there is a plan here, there is a strategy...We just need to let it unfold, you and me – together. Like the good old pals we have always been."

Butterflies flittered in his stomach. He was on edge, nervous; it wasn't the nice kind of butterflies – it was an anxious, depleted-wreck kind of butterflies. He had no other option but to trust this specter in front of him, who was coercing him into insanity at every possible avenue.

"Fine! I'll *cooperate*. This isn't the first time you've said that, too. How many sugars do you take?"

"I like my coffee the same way I like my people: sweet and innocent. I'll take two and a half, please."

"And you said you wanted a biscuit with that?"

"If it would be possible."

"Sure. I mean, anything's possible, right?"

"You really are a sweetheart – do you know that, Davie boy? *Anything's possible*. That's exactly right. News should be coming on at around five o'clock, maybe we should watch it for any updates on this alleged night prowler."

"Maybe..." said David, still plagued by anxious thoughts about his wife.

They sat together, just looking at each other, for half an hour while Carter slurped on his coffee. The television muttered in the background.

Finally, as the news began, they both turned their eyes to the television, each as highly alert as the other.

"Good evening, San Francisco," said the anchorman. "Things have not been looking so good in Golden Gate Park down by Stow Lake, where several women have reportedly been found dead. The police have been gathering evidence and even have a suspect in custody, but whether or not they can prove it was him still remains a mystery. In other news—"

Carter used the remote control to turn off the television. "See, pal. They've got a suspect and it's not you, it's not us, it's not me."

"Doesn't prove a damn thing. Why is Sarah still missing then? They've got the wrong suspect."

Agent Carter was familiar with the concept of mirroring: copying the behavior of another person to make them feel validated and understood. "Maybe…" he said, in the exact same way David had said it, leaving David even more convinced that they had the wrong person in custody.

David went back to fond memories of him and Sarah. When things were good. Holding her close as they sat in peaceful nature. Growing plants together in the garden. The times when they'd talked away the few hours they had together during the day. She'd been a pretty young woman, too. But what was of utmost importance was that they never lied to each other.

Now, there were two possible scenarios: either she was dead or she had left him for someone else. And if she was going to leave him for someone else, she would have told him straight up. So, there was only one conclusion for David. The night prowler, whoever he was, had got her.

His eyes became cloudy with tears again. Carter watched him struggle.

"Hey, pal, it's alright," he said softly. "We'll find the truth."

David exploded. "Shut up! Just shut up, alright? She's dead!"

"This anger of yours worries me, David."

"Why?"

"Because if you get this angry over nothing, imagine what you could have been like with her."

David's milky eyes simply gazed into the distance. "Yeah…" he said. "You're probably right – yeah."

"Was there ever a time when you just exploded for no reason?"

"Well, I wouldn't be able to tell you, I don't remember much when I explode."

"See that's the problem, if you lose time and forget what happens in a fit of rage – well, uh, let's just say we may have a reason to believe it could have been you."

"And are you certain of that? Please, Agent Carter, just tell me the truth."

"Certain? Certainty can be a symptom of a little thing that's known as 'confirmation bias.' You ever heard of that one, David?"

"I can't say I have."

"Well, look at you, taking every little thing I say, every sign you get from your perception of the outside world, everything you know – or rather, uh, *think* you know about yourself and twisting it and meshing it all together until you have no option but to be certain that you did it. But your certainty is subjective. Reality is objective, David – and unfortunately, subjectivity just doesn't cut it for me."

"So, there is no truth here?"

"Who said there was no truth?"

"You did, just now – you said that objectivity has basically just gone out the window for me."

"There is a grain of truth in every lie, David."

David just frowned. "Son of a bitch," he said, frustrated with Carter and his riddles. "When are you just going to talk straight with me? I know you know something – just come clean!"

"Come clean with what, David? *Know?* What do I know? What does anybody know? Please, David, I don't want to start getting into the philosophy of knowing and certainty. The truth is I'm just a guy who's trying to help. Trying to help you find your wife. But the pieces, they won't always fit. We need to keep trying to assemble this huge puzzle we have before us without making any rushed judgments. Without making assumptions. We need to stick to what's real."

"I don't know what's real anymore!"

"That's because you keep rushing to make assumptions! Is that my fault or yours?"

"You're right. You're right. Everything's my fault – this is all on me."

"Thank you!"

"Yeah, but what exactly have you done to help or make it better?"

"David, David! I showed you where to begin with this giant jigsaw puzzle! When you've got a thousand puzzle pieces in front of you, where do you start? The middle? The right corner, the left corner? I pointed you in the right direction!" said Carter, tapping his index finger emphatically on the coffee table.

David looked away, rubbing his lower lip with his thumb as he thought it over. "Right…" he said, his voice a mere whisper.

"So, you agree?"

"Yeah – yeah, I agree."

"Excellent…"

"So, where do we go from here?"

"We're like a train, going in a straight line," said Carter, cunning as always. "Let's verge to another side for a little while."

"What do you mean by that?"

"Well, I'm your old pal, Agent Carter. Let's just talk about life."

"Talk about life? My life has become unbearable."

"Don't think too much about that now. Tell me, David – if we could guarantee her safety, what would you say your outlook on life would be?"

"I'd say it would be the same it's always been. Work hard, provide, be grateful for each moment I spend with her. If she knocked on that door right now, I would be the happiest man in the world. I would even accept her request to have a kid or two and just find another part-time job to bring in more income. My outlook? Life would be beautiful again."

"And what if she was in a casket?"

"Agent Carter…please…Don't."

"Well, you've got to account for both sides!"

"I can't account for that. That would kill me. I would die of heartache."

"You would cease to exist."

"Yeah."

"I can't begin to say how sorry I am for the situation you're in…" said Carter.

"You? Sorry?" David scoffed. "Yeah, right."

"No, I'm being serious." Carter gazed at him like a shark. "You have no idea."

"So, you…*care* about me? Is that what you're saying?"

"In some ways I do. Ways you wouldn't understand."

"I don't know what that means and I don't want to know what that means."

"I'm glad."

"Why?"

"Because the *truth* is something you can't handle yet. That's my opinion at least."

David was out of words to say. Reality seemed to slip from his grasp.

Carter would have made an excellent chess player. Tactical, vicious, always one step ahead. And poor David, the simple kind of man – it's not even like he walked into Carter's trap. Carter had brutally imposed himself on him, and because simple men are vulnerable men, his line of defense just kept getting weaker.

"Right," said David.

"Turn on the TV," ordered Carter. "There must be some kind of update about the serial killer."

David did as he was told, turning the station to the news channel. They were broadcasting about something else, but on the ticker were the headlines about the San Francisco massacres. "*Suspect released from custody – no substantial evidence to prove his guilt.*"

"Oh dear," said Carter, feigning concern.

David's mind started to spiral out of control. Perspiration appeared on his forehead; he was flushed, certainty taken from him yet again. This horrible man who had forced his way into his life had filled his head with insane little ideas – and he did it by proxy. All those insane little ideas were put there by David himself.

He started fantasizing again. Started thinking those dark, dark thoughts again. Blaming himself. All it would take was an outburst of rage, or to not be fully present inside his own body, his own mind – which, as Carter pointed out, could be a move David had made on the chessboard of life.

"That's it," said David, resolutely. "I'm handing myself in to the police. I know I'm the one who's responsible for this."

"You're a diamond," was Carter's response. "Shimmering brightly. I think I'll let you do it this time."

"Is your car parked outside?"

"Yes."

"Could you drive me to the station?"

"I'll accompany you there, yes."

The police station was about a twenty-minute drive. David sighed a profound sigh, a mixture of guilt and anxiety, as they parked outside.

"You sure you want to do this?" asked Carter coolly.

"Well, what other option do I have?"

"Well, okay. Let's go inside."

David trudged into the station as if he already had shackles around his ankles. People were waiting to talk to the officer on duty, but David skipped the queue and went to the cubicle. It was shut off by metal bars and had a plastic protector and a small hole to talk to the policewoman behind the desk.

"I need to turn myself in for a crime," he told her.

"What did you do?" she asked, a certain superiority mixed with her curiosity.

"The murders, down by Stow Lake. I think that was me."

"What do you mean you *think* that was you? Was it you or not?" she replied, more intense this time.

"I just think it was me."

"Okay. Are you with him?" she said, pointing to Carter.

"Yeah."

"Both of you are going to need to come in for questioning. Did you bring him here, are y'all together?"

"Yes ma'am," said Carter, calmly.

"Okay." She pushed a red button and a door opened, leading to the back of the station.

Both Carter and David were to be rigorously interrogated, but Carter took it in his stride as if nothing could go wrong for him. David, on the other hand, was petrified.

They were interrogated separately. David found himself sitting across from a detective, a burly man with a ponytail, both of them with their arms resting on a metal table. There was a camera recording the interrogation and a tape recorder keeping track of David's words.

For a big, strong man, the detective had a higher-pitched voice than expected. He began by asking David who he was, what he did for a living, how old he was and whether or not he had committed any crimes in the past. Pretty straightforward questions. But when the detective asked him why he had handed himself in to the police, things got a little more complicated.

"It's my wife, Sarah. She hasn't been home since last night and I didn't see her during the day either because I was at work."

"What does your wife have to do with this?"

"Well, I think I'm the one behind the killings. I think I freaked out, had a fit of rage, killed her and then just blanked out and forgot everything. Same with the other women."

"Sir, that could be a possibility – but these killings are more meticulous than I can go into. Whoever's behind them is a sharp-minded individual. He kills in a pattern, dismembers the bodies in the same way – he's an artist, actually, in his own sick way, and I just don't think you're that type of person."

"So, why haven't I seen Sarah for two days?"

"There could be simpler reasons."

"How do you know that when I blank out I don't turn into this 'artist,' as you put it."

"I can't know that for sure, you are right. But we've found no traces of the killer's DNA anywhere near the bodies. If you were half-asleep, so to speak, wouldn't you think that you'd be sloppy? Leave traces behind?"

David began to calm down, though anxiety still gripped him. He exhaled gently through his nose.

The detective picked up on his emotional state. "Sir, are you having any personal issues in your life right now that might make you think irrationally? It's not every day a serial killer of this caliber just hands himself in, do you agree?"

"I don't know...I guess so."

"So, what's been going on?"

"Well, I was twelve thousand dollars overdue on taxes, and this guy called Agent Carter just turned up at my house and had my car taken away from me."

"We're interviewing Carter in another room. Is there anything else you'd like to say about him? Has he caused you any stress, maybe? Has he been bothering you?"

"He's been asking a lot of questions, let's just put it that way."

"Questions about what?"

"Sarah."

"So, do you think he's doing this because he wants to help?"

"That's what he claims, I guess."

"Sir, when you came here, did you come looking for help? I mean, some kind of assistance with, maybe, a psychiatrist? Or do you think, maybe, it's all just the stress of the tax issue and whatnot that's causing you to, maybe, act out of the ordinary?"

"I – I don't know. I guess, maybe the whole 'twelve thousand dollars overdue,' as Carter keeps saying, put me under enough stress to make me feel *edgy*. You know. Like there was something wrong with me."

"Alright, David. Well, thanks for coming in, it was very brave of you, but we just don't have the evidence we need to arrest you for something as serious as this. We're experts on the matter – we know what we're doing, and I know I'm right when

I tell you you're not the one who did this. Listen though, if you ever need anything, take down my number. I'll be more than happy to offer you some comfort in this tempest you are facing with your missing wife, and if you need any psychological assistance, we can get you in touch with a professional."

David felt a cathartic flow wash through him. "Thank you, detective."

So, what happened during Carter's interrogation? It was the same setup: the camera, the tape recorder. He was relaxed, undid a couple of buttons on his shirt. He was being interrogated by a slightly more slender man, with neat black hair and a pale face.

"So, you brought him here," said the detective. "Why does he say he killed those women?"

"Detective, let me be clear with you. I've, uh, been dealing with his mood swings for two days now, and let's just say he isn't the most stable guy. He's got a good side to him though, I'll grant him that, but I think it comes down to one thing: twelve thousand dollars overdue. We had to seize his car. Then there's the problem with the wife. He thinks he's killed her because he has these anger fits that he claims make him forget what happens after he's had one – but I wouldn't take that too seriously, happens to a lot of men. And seeing as he's probably got a mortgage over his head and a low wage, he can't give his wife kids because he can't afford it – who can blame him?"

"That was informative on your behalf…I thank you for that. But what's your role in all this?"

"Me? I'm here to keep him sane! The man is losing touch with reality! Everybody in this goddamn station knows he didn't kill those women! Something's going on with him, and I need to look after him."

"Don't you think that should be the job of a mental health specialist?"

"He needs a friend, detective. And most of all…he needs love. A shrink isn't going to show him any love. Right now, I'm all he's got. Now, I don't know what he's said about me in the other room, but I'm pretty sure that he knows I'm here for him.

Here to help him." Carter said this knowing full well that David was not capable of escaping his conditioning.

"Right, okay," said the detective. "And what about the lake? Do you have any comments on that?"

"No comment whatsoever. You guys have a tough job on your hands. Whoever's out there killing those women is sure outsmarting you guys right now, that's for sure."

"Right. Okay, *thanks* for that. I think it's about time you got out of here."

"I'm clear to go?"

"You're clear."

Carter got up, swished his blazer over his shoulder and waltzed out of that room feeling like a million-dollar man.

CHAPTER 5

On the journey back to David's house, Carter simply whistled and lightly caressed the steering wheel. He said nothing to David until they were approaching his house, when he asked, coughing the words out: "So, did you fool them pretty good?"

"F-fool them? What do you mean, fool them? I told them the truth about everything. I didn't lie once."

"Oh, so you're in the clear then?"

"I'm what?"

"In the clear. They don't suspect you at all?"

"They asked me if I needed any psychological help. The detective even gave me his number, said if I ever needed to talk to someone he'd be there for me."

"Ah, I wouldn't trust them too much."

"Why not?"

"They're always pinning things down on innocent people – and, uh, you're innocent, aren't you, David?"

David chuckled. "Hah. I guess so!"

"Yeah, keep guessing, see where that takes you."

"What does that mean?"

"What I'm saying is we can't trust a word they said! The police know they're good-for-nothing fools – otherwise, they would have caught the guy by now!"

"So, let me get this straight…After all that – you're still not going to let me give up on the idea that it was me?"

"You can do whatever you want with your *ideas* – they belong to you, don't they? Don't you have a mind of your own?"

David still couldn't see through him. He still couldn't see how much Carter had stolen from him. "Alright, I never said anything wrong. Jeez, calm down."

"What did the detective tell you about the killer?"

"Said he was an 'artist' – good at what he does, in other words. They can't trace him."

"And what about you when you were talking to him? Do you think you were good at talking to him?"

"I just told him the truth."

"The truth?"

"Yeah. I told you, I never lied once."

"The worst type of lie is when people lie to themselves, David. Remember that. When you start lying to yourself – well – uh, that's when you really start losing your grip on reality."

"What's that supposed to mean?"

"Can I ask you a question?"

"Um…sure."

"How would you dispose of a dead body and hide the evidence, if you were a serial killer?"

"I really have no idea."

"You see, it's weird you would say that. Any normal person would try to answer that question, however ridiculous and stupid they would sound – you know, just for gags – but you, you just *don't know*, do you?"

"No, I don't."

"So, there's a blank there – a gap, so to speak."

"Oh, I see. So, you've started with your little riddles again."

Carter put on a silly voice and said, "Fooled 'em pretty good!"

"Fooled who, Agent Carter? The police? They're professionals, they know exactly what they're doing and they knew exactly who they were up against when they interviewed me in that room. I'm not the killer. End of."

"And you're certain of that, are you?"

"I'm certain."

"I hate that word. The idea of certainty. Everything's solid as a rock, isn't it? Written in stone. Just like it was before we came to the station, when you were convinced you hacked up women and threw them in a lake; now you're certain it wasn't you. *Certainty.* You know, there's a brain disease where the sufferer could swear bugs are living inside their skin and they scratch away at it, but they're the only one that can see them? And when you try to convince them that they don't exist, it only makes the ideation worse?"

"I couldn't give a damn about what you have to say. Now let me out of this car, since we're near my place, and go away."

"You ought to be ashamed of yourself, talking to your old friend Agent Carter that way."

"I've known you for two days!"

"Hey! Don't you start with that! You admitted yourself you've felt like you've known me for longer!"

"Known you for longer, huh? What does that mean, *known you for longer*?"

"Now you're asking the right type of question."

"I've known you since Sarah went missing."

"That's right – bingo! Since Sarah went missing. Doesn't it seem a little odd to you that the mail had just arrived, and I came in the very same day the letter was sent?"

"So, what are you implying now? That you're a figment of my imagination again?"

"Could be that I'm just a diligent tax agent."

"So, is this all just you trying to prove that nothing's certain? Because, for some reason, you keep questioning certainty, and I don't know whether it's just some sick little joke or you studied a philosophy elective in college or something and can't let go of the idea."

"*Certainty.*" He shook his head. "Stinks like the mouth of a whore."

"I see – so this is all *you*, then. It's always been about you."

"David, we have merely put ten per cent of the jigsaw puzzle together. Do you know how much further we have to go?"

"To find Sarah? That's the police's job, buddy, not yours."

"No, not to find Sarah. To find *you*, David, to find you."

Carter parked outside David's house. David opened the door, got out, and Carter just sped away without saying another word. David wasn't sure he'd see him the next day, or ever again for that matter, and he'd left him with yet another riddle he couldn't understand.

"To find me..." he muttered as he unlocked his front door. "To find me."

He did feel slightly relieved that Carter had left, but it was short-lived. When he turned on the television, Sarah's name came up as one of the missing women. This made him feel extremely depressed and anxious, and on top of this, the doubt that Carter had left him with about the nature of reality – his reality – was gnawing at him in the back of his mind.

He paced up and down the house until about three in the morning, when, finally, he collapsed into a black nothingness. And that scared him. He had no idea what would happen in that nothingness.

See, Carter had planted a seed and watered it plenty. David was scared of the dark – the dark inside him, the darkness in his consciousness; he was afraid that he wasn't fully in control, but at the same time he craved it, that break from reality.

For the first time in years, he dreamed. He dreamed about the bodies of those murdered women; he felt himself present in the location of their deaths; he felt *responsible*.

At about six, he woke up, heart racing, but no trace of blood anywhere, no trace that he had left the house. He thanked his lucky stars it was only a bad dream and took a walk outside, passing by Papa Greg's house (without knowing it was Papa Greg), who just stared him down with a really mean look on his face, confusing David even more.

He returned to his house for breakfast, keeping the television on at all times for any updates about Sarah.

"Oh, darling..." he said, tears appearing in his eyes again. "Where have you gone?"

It was at that very moment that he heard Carter's car sputtering outside. He recognized it by the sound it made, the way he aggressively slammed his car door, and then the ringing of his doorbell.

David became frustrated. "Damn it."

He opened the door nonetheless and looked Carter directly in the eye, trying to figure out what mood he was in. Whether he had come to play games with his mind again, or whether he was here to be his old pal from way back, offering him a helping hand in this time of need. He couldn't make out anything, and Carter barged in, inviting himself into David's house, a place where he had now made himself comfortable.

"So, have you done any soul-searching in my brief absence?" asked Carter. "Can't leave you on your own for too long, never know what might happen."

"Morning…" said David in a husky, beat-up tone, eyes full of doubt.

Carter started laughing again, a giggling, wheezing laugh. "Morning, he says! Yes, David, morning, indeed!"

"So, you're back for more. More of whatever it is you say."

"I'm not the kind of guy to abandon a friend, especially in tough times."

"Not just any friend," confirmed David sarcastically, "your old friend."

"I see you're still glued to the television. Looking for answers in the wrong places again. Ever heard the phrase 'he who looks outside sleeps, he who looks inside awakens'?"

"Can't say I have."

"Famous quote by a famous doctor of psychology. Carl Jung," said Carter with enthusiasm.

"Good for you."

"Sleep well, David?"

"Cup of coffee, Agent Carter?" David raised his voice louder than Carter's.

"Did – you – sleep – well – last – night?" repeated Carter, syllable by syllable.

"Had a dream for the first time in years."

"What did you dream of? Meadows and pretty little butterflies?"

"If you must know, I dreamt I was down by Stow Lake, among the bodies of the women that have been killed."

"Well, what a coincidence."

"Doesn't mean a damn thing. You know how much this has impacted me. You know how scared I am for Sarah."

"Was it a vivid dream? How present were you?"

"Present enough."

"Present enough for what? Present enough to say that maybe it wasn't all in your head?"

"If I was anywhere near Stow Lake, the patrol vehicles would have arrested me by now."

"Doesn't mean a damn thing," said Carter, mirroring David. "Could have been a memory from when this all started."

"The police said it wasn't me! How much more evidence do you need?"

"Police are idiots. Wasn't it you who said they were dealing with an 'artist'?"

"I don't think I've ever had it in me to be an 'artist' at killing innocent women."

"How does a man turn into a monster without knowing it?"

"Oh, you and your psychobabble bullcrap."

"Think about it, David. Think about your *life* for a second."

"What about my life?"

"Well, it's bad enough you had to resign from your government job to work at a plastic recycling factory with a lower wage, a lower quality of life. But what if, throughout all this, you have developed a deep-seated hatred for women? Not something you have control over, of course. Something your conscious mind won't allow you to believe. I mean, I know you said you love Sarah and all, but at the end of the day – how much do you really love her? Don't you think the fact that your marriage has become stagnant because you can't afford the life-style she wants and you can't give her children because of your overall impotence – hasn't that turned it inwards on you and begun festering there like a puss-filled boil?"

"You mean, I can't admit to myself that I hate women?"

"What gender is your manager at the factory?"

"She's a woman."

"Well, there you go. I bet she does a hell of a lot of nagging. And what gender gave you the most hell at your government job? Who gossiped and spread nasty rumors about you the most?"

"Well…the majority of them were women…You're right."

"Exactly, David. And that leaves us with one objective fact: we are uncovering an unconscious misogyny in you!"

"How the hell do you know? Are you a psychiatrist or something? No, you're a tax man! Supposedly!"

"Doesn't mean I haven't read a book or two about this sort of thing."

"Oh. So, you're an *educated* bureaucratic bastard!"

"And when your dad came home drunk and beat your mother, do you think he had any legitimate reasons for doing so?"

"I really don't know. I was too young to know."

"Another blank space, waiting to be discovered."

"And who's talking? The tax man, the fed or the figment of my imagination?"

"If you're too uncertain to know that – uh – there's nothing I can do to help you."

"Alright, I'll assume you're a figment of my imagination, then! Just to make you happy! And I'll also assume that this figment of my imagination knows more about me than I do! How's that? You happy now?"

"Maybe you took yourself to the police station, maybe the cups of coffee you make me – maybe you're the one drinking them. Maybe you're so deluded, everything you do with me is just a mirage shimmering in the desert sand."

David felt the blood rush to his head. "There we go, you're real happy!"

"*Twelve thousand dollars overdue.*"

"And there's the catchphrase!"

"You're like a red diamond," said Carter. "Did you know those are the rarest ones?"

"Oh yeah?" David was fuming now. "And what if I beat your ass?"

"Then you would be beating up an imaginary person. The only thing you'd accomplish is breaking all the furniture in your kitchen and living room."

David was just posturing anyway. He could never "beat his ass;" he couldn't beat anybody's ass. He gave up on the idea pretty quickly and returned to his familiar state of defeated depression, with his drooping, drowsy eyes to showcase it. Carter saw that he had won, yet again, and a big, beaming grin appeared on his face, shining onto David.

"So, what do I do now?" said David. "Admit that I'm a misogynist? Have you drive me to the police station again and tell them about the dream I had last night, and try to convince them it wasn't just a dream?"

"They'll lock you up in the psych ward."

"Yeah, then it'll just be you and me talking to each other, forever. Won't it, Agent Carter?"

"Well, if that's what you want then, I mean, it can be arranged. But I'll be out of your hair soon enough, don't worry, David."

"How soon?"

"That hasn't been decided yet."

David muttered a few curse words under his breath. "Well, what do you want from me, then?"

"How about another coffee?"

"Who's going to be drinking it, you or me? That hasn't been decided yet either, has it?"

"Two and a half sugars and a biscuit. It's too early in the morning to decide anything, I'm afraid."

"Oh yeah, what are we waiting for then? Sarah to come back?" David's eyes glistened with tears. "And don't you dare tell me she's fine where she is!"

"David?"

"Yes?"

"Coffee."

"Make it yourself! Everything's right there in the kitchen. I guess I'll just be hallucinating you making it!"

"That's not how we treat our guests."

"Alright, fine! I'll make you a damn coffee!"

"Thank you."

David went to the kitchen counter and boiled the water. "Yeah, and I'll be asking the damn questions from now on."

He stirred the instant coffee and sugar in Carter's mug violently, annoyed he had to keep making coffee for this uninvited "guest."

"You want to ask someone you believe to be an imaginary person – uh – questions?"

"Well, I might as well get to know my alter ego better!"

Carter, for the first time ever, gave in to this request with neutrality. "Fine, fire away."

"You said you've been married several times. To who? And did you have any children?"

"My first wife's name was Emma. We had two children, Jack and Jill. Jack and Jill went up the hill to fetch a pail of water. Jack fell down and broke his crown, and Jill came tumbling after."

David exhaled angrily. "Here's your goddamn coffee," he said, handing him the mug. "It's all games with you isn't it, Agent Carter?"

"Well, don't you want to know about my second marriage?"

"Another nursery rhyme, is it?"

"Met me a pretty little girl named Mia, married her and had a kid called Jack – uh, again. Little Jack Horner sat in a corner, eating a Christmas pie. He put in his thumb and pulled out a plum and said, 'What a good boy am I!'"

"Son of a bitch."

"What, am I not satisfying you? Does your alter ego need to be more complex? Do you have the capacity, do you think, to come up with something more complex?"

"I think you're about as complex as they get."

A twinkle emerged in Carter's eyes. "You know, for someone who thinks he's delusional, you're still quite intelligent."

"Thank you. Now, if you don't mind, you can shut up now, I'm turning up the TV."

"I'll seal my mouth and throw away the key!"

David turned his attention back to the news channel, praying that Sarah had been found alive somewhere, managed to escape the bloodshed down by the lake – though dead women were popping up in different locations now, with the police reporting that it was still the same killer because of the terrible way they had been killed. Sarah had not been found dead but was still on the missing persons list.

David sighed a big, heavy sigh, wishing there was still hope. Carter mirrored David's behavior and sighed along with him, but then he couldn't help himself from smirking and letting out a little chuckle.

"You think this is *funny?*" asked David in horror.

"Of course not, I was thinking about something else."

"What were you thinking about?"

"Forget it."

"You're lying! You think this is a joke, you sick bastard!"

"Well, if I think this is a joke, that means you think this is a joke, too. Except, if I'm your alter ego, then we're different subpersonalities split apart pretty widely from each other, aren't we?"

"How do you know all this *crap*, all this psychobabble *bullcrap?*"

"I told you. I've read a book or two in my life. You may have read the same books when you went into hiding during the time you were being bullied at your government job, who knows?"

"So, you think that's what caused the original crack in my personality?"

"Finally." Carter exhaled in relief. "A sane question. I told you, David, we need to find *you*. And once we've found you, we'll find Sarah, too."

"So, I'm sick? Sick in the head? Is that what you're saying?"

"Please, speak about yourself with a little more compassion. But the bottom line is, yes. Now, just how sick you are? Let's just say there's a spectrum for that – and I might not be on that spectrum. At all."

"But aren't you the one convincing me you're my alter ego? That we are one thing, just split apart?"

"*Twelve thousand dollars overdue.*"

"So, you're a tax man again now?"

"The jigsaw puzzle, David, is far more complex than you think. It's got different layers, different dimensions. Maybe you think I've got all the answers, and I just don't. Maybe neither of us do. Maybe this situation is far more difficult than either of us can anticipate."

"Alright, let's stick to the topic. I'm sick, right?"

"Your upbringing, David. Your father was an alcoholic who beat your mother…Some kids go insane for far less than that. But you're a tough old walnut, aren't you? Let me tell you something though…even the toughest walnuts can be cracked."

"What else?"

"The mundane days at the factory melting plastic, the financial pressure, the pressure from Sarah to have kids and you not being able to. You cracked, man – you're toasted, your brain is fried!"

"And how do you know that if…you're me?"

"Maybe I'm a part of yourself reaching out to you, man! Or maybe I'm not you at all – but if you can't tell the difference between yourself and someone else then, like I've said countless times, you're cracked beyond help."

"If you're just a part of me, and she's not back by tomorrow, I'll hang myself in this kitchen! You hear me, you son of a bitch? Then you'll die, too, if you really are my alter ego!"

"And what if I'm not? What if Sarah comes back the day after to see you swinging from a noose? Then what? You'd risk it all that easily? That means you're impulsive, too!"

"Another diagnosis! Now I'm impulsive!"

"Well, you are. I mean, after what you just said, that can't be disputed."

"So, who's the one killing women if I'm so impulsive, you or me? Because if you're me and I'm you, one of us has to be doing it!"

"Oh, Sarah's fine!" said Carter, frustrated.

"I told you not to pull that 'Sarah's fine' crap on me again, because I don't know what it means! Just like I don't know what ninety-nine per cent of the crap that comes out your mouth means!"

"You're hanging over the edge of a cliff, do you know that, David?"

"That's *your fault!*" yelled David.

"Oh, here we go again, projecting all your negativity onto me."

"*Projecting?* Projecting! You're just a psychobabble ency-clopedia, aren't you? What was that government psy-op you talked about a few days ago? Project MK-Ultra or whatever? Let me tell you something, pal – if you're a government agent who's been sent down here to drive me crazy, first of all, I'm not going to let it work! Second, that's technically illegal! So, I can just have you arrested, how about that?"

"My name is Agent Carter, I am your tax agent, and I am simply trying to help."

"So, you're a tax agent, you son of a bitch?" said David, get-ting closer to Carter's face. He paused for a second, his para-noia rising up from the depths. "That's something my alter ego would say..."

Carter's lips twitched into a smile. "Oh, David..."

CHAPTER 6

David's tragic flaw was that he wouldn't let himself win. It was one of those unconscious things Carter talked about. Carter, being the predator he was, knew this, too. He knew he had dug the sword deep into David's guts. That no matter what happened, he was always the puppeteer and the mastermind – leading David fast down a path that led straight over a cliff.

David was hanging on to his sanity by a thread. He had no idea who or what Carter was, so Carter made him believe he was switching roles – the tax man, the alter ego, the fed – because Carter didn't want to wake him up to the truth yet. The truth, not only too hard to handle, was something Carter wanted to slowly release David into after he was done playing with him. Even though, as an entity, he wanted to destroy David, he'd grown fond of him, fond of how easy a target he was, and he was amused by this.

"I just want to end it all," said David, confused and disoriented.

"I – uh – really can't let you do that, buddy. Don't make me call the psych ward. If I tell them about the conversations we've had, you'll be a lifer. And then it could really just be you and me in a padded cell for the rest of your life. Even I don't want that."

"Why do you keep doing this? Whatever it is you're doing."

"Well, some people could call it gaslighting."

"What's gaslighting?"

"It's when you lie to someone to the point where they start to doubt their own reality."

"Right. Right…" said David, who couldn't believe that, even though Carter had admitted what he was doing, he still couldn't break free.

"But it's not gaslighting if it's the truth! And I swear on my bones, I have never once lied to you. In fact, I would say I've been so honest with you that I've shattered all of your illusions."

"Shattered my illusions – yeah, because before you came along, everything was an illusion, wasn't it? My home was an illusion, my job was an illusion, my relationship with my wife… everything was just a lie I was telling myself."

"Absolutely."

"And you're here to tell me the *truth* about myself."

"There's no point resisting it, David."

Pain erupted along David's every nerve, sharp and sudden. He crouched down on the floor and tipped over into fetal position, pulling at his hair and wailing out. Tears streamed from his eyes. "Sarah!" he screamed. "Just come back! Somebody, please help me, I'm losing my friggin' mind!"

Carter crouched down beside him and patted him gently on the shoulder, "There, there. Leave it to your old friend Agent Carter. We'll get Sarah back, I promise. And as soon as you start learning to accept the truth…well, you won't be in so much pain anymore, will you?"

"There's no use in asking who you are!" he screamed. "There's no use in asking you where Sarah is! All you do is lie!"

"David, I've told you who I am multiple times – I'm your old pal Agent Carter, your tax agent. Now you know that, don't you?"

"No, I goddamn don't! I don't know if you're real or not!"

"Well—"

"Well, what? If that's the way it is, there's nothing you can do to help me. You've said that over and over again! Please, just take me to the ward!"

"If I take you to the ward, they'll turn you into a human experiment, you fool!"

"But isn't that exactly what I am right now? Just one of your experiments?"

"David, have I ever asked you for anything other than a cup of coffee and a biscuit, whilst we sit here watching the news, looking out for Sarah? Have I asked you for money, even with what you owe the government? Have I ever done anything that proves empirically that I am out to get you? Have I ever threatened you with violence? You're paranoid, man! Get a grip on yourself!"

While he took in what Carter was saying, David rocked himself back and forth until he'd stopped blubbering like a baby. Then he just lay there.

"Stand up, man!" said Carter. "And stand tall!"

David got up from the floor and wiped the tears from his eyes.

"Now, shake my hand," said Carter, in a truly masculine tone. David shook his hand. "We're in this together."

"This isn't one of your tricks?" asked David.

"Of course not, David. You know how far back me and you go – uh, metaphorically speaking. I just want to help."

"Alright," said David. "Alright. *Whoever you are,* you just want to help. I get it now. I get it."

"Alright. When was the last time you had a shave and shower? Looked after yourself a little bit? Changed your clothes?"

"Since…since Sarah went missing."

"Okay, well, I suggest you do that. I'll turn the TV on and switch it to the news channel. If anything happens, I'll let you know."

"Alright, thanks, Agent Carter. I'll be down in about twenty minutes."

"Take as much time as you need."

"Alright, thank you."

Carter switched over to MTV and turned the volume down so David wouldn't be able to make out what he was watching. As soon as he heard him clumping down the stairs, he switched straight back to the news channel, changed his posture and said, "David, things aren't looking too good; the police say it's only a matter of time until they find all the bodies. The women on the missing persons list may as well be considered dead. This guy – he's not fooling around. The police have warned anyone with a family member considered missing to expect the worst."

David rested his head on the wall and thumped it with his fist. He stayed there for a while, more tears rising to the surface, but he tried to hold them back, knowing that crying so much wasn't the manly thing to do. "So, what do we do now?"

Carter looked like he was all out of ideas. "I'm sorry, pal," he said, making it clear he believed Sarah was dead and there was nothing else to be done. He straightened up his tie, put his blazer on and looked like he was about to leave through the front door.

"W-wait! Agent Carter! Where are you going?"

"We've got to admit she's dead. There's nothing else I can do for you, I'm afraid. I've done everything I can. Thanks for the company, pal. Oh and – uh – the coffee."

"Wait, I thought you said we were in this together, that we would do whatever it takes to find Sarah! You can't just leave me here!"

"I still remember all the times you've begged me to leave you be," said Carter, faking a kind of nostalgia.

"Carter—"

"*Agent* Carter."

"Agent Carter, I need you!"

Carter paused for a moment. His back was to David, but he had a huge grin on his face. He felt like giggling again, but now was too critical a time. "Alright, pal. But like I said a few times before, you need to start being more cooperative."

"I'll cooperate!"

"Good." Carter hid his smile and turned back around. "Let's get down to business."

They sat down in the living room facing each other again. Carter seemed serious.

"How come you wanted to walk out on me like that?" asked David, concerned.

"I just figured this whole thing was a waste of time."

"Waste of time? In what way? You said we were going to find Sarah."

"Well, you see, I've spent a lot of time with you, David, and – uh – I just don't think we're going to come to any rational sort of conclusion here. Your mind's a mess. I figured, just let the cops deal with it, they'll catch whoever's behind this eventually. See, I think by spending some time away from you, we can study those moments where you go blank, see if we can – you know – put two and two together."

"Moments when I go blank?"

"Yeah, at about three in the morning – isn't that when you usually sleep?"

"I never said that."

"But you did, you just don't remember telling me."

"Right…" David was confused and concerned, but he wasn't quite sure what Carter was getting at yet.

"Do you – uh – have the faintest idea of what blood smells like?"

"No idea whatsoever."

"Another blank in the mind. Come on, David, do you really expect me to believe that? Look, you've cut yourself shaving – can you wipe the scratch with your finger and then smell the blood?"

David did as he was asked. "Smells…kind of metallic."

"That would be the iron in it. Does that smell bring back any memories?"

"Well, what kind of memory is it supposed to bring back?"

"The kind of memory you won't allow yourself to remember."

Carter had gone back into fed mode. David knew what he was implying, but he wasn't sure what to do. What if he was the "artist"? Would he turn himself in? Or were the feds just waiting to pin this on someone innocent, someone damaged like him?

"I have no idea what you're talking about."

"See, that's what I thought you'd say. So how about I give you a chance to freshen up your mind, and we'll see what happens when you drift into oblivion tonight."

"What, you think I go blank and kill them in my sleep?" said David, desperately hoping Carter would give him a straight answer for once.

"Try not going to sleep tonight, and we'll just see what's on the news tomorrow. If there aren't any fresh kills, well, then... who knows? But nothing is certain. Remember what I told you about certainty? That word repulses me."

"Alright, we'll work this out. I'll fight off the sleep. Look, Agent Carter...if it is me...then I'm willing to accept the consequences for it. Just know that."

"How noble. Can I leave now?"

"Yes. Yes, you can leave."

"See you tomorrow."

"Yeah. See you tomorrow."

David sighed miserably as he watched Carter go. He closed the front door and let the battle with himself begin.

It wasn't the battle to stay awake that bothered him. That was the easy part. The tough part was staying inside himself without losing his mind.

He sat in complete stillness for a couple of hours, with no sounds around him other than passing cars outside, and sipped at a coffee that had cooled down too much. He thought about the very first evening he met Agent Carter and anything else that may have happened that day to cause Sarah to go missing. The truth was, they'd bickered at breakfast about not being able to have any children – something that was, as we know, an ongoing argument between them.

He remained still, a train of memories – the good times, the bad times, unraveling the past twenty years, thinking about Carter's theory that he'd become bitter and misogynistic, not knowing what to believe, whether it made sense or not – and for about two or three hours he sat on the couch with the TV switched off, staring blankly at the black screen without a single positive emotion cropping up among the holocaust of his existence, until something happened. He could hear the jingling of keys rattling on a keychain and someone unlocking the front door. His heart started beating at a wild pace, but he remained firm on the couch, expecting the unexpected, not able to move.

He managed to squeeze out a couple of words in his heightened adrenalized state. "Who's there?"

Stillness. There was no answer but a creaking door.

He finally found the courage to get up and go see for himself. What he saw brought him to his knees.

"Oh my god…Oh my god – Sarah…"

His face went pale as a sheet of paper. He was almost about to collapse at her feet, but she quickly put an end to any sentimentality.

"That's right, I'm back." She threw her belongings on the floor and tied her shoulder-length brown hair into a knot behind her head.

"D-darling, you're back. But w-what's the matter?"

"I was too busy to watch any news the first few days I was gone, but after I saw that you had declared me missing, I had to come back as a matter of principle. But nothing more."

His heart fractured into a million tiny pieces. This was not what he'd expected at all. He needed a loving embrace, a kiss. He wanted her to hold him until they melted into each other, reunited at last. But her mood would not allow it.

"Where have you been?" He almost choked on the words.

"Scott's house," she said, firmly and angrily.

"Scott? Which Scott? You mean the doctor?"

"Yes."

"But why?"

"If you must know, we've been having an affair."

He felt a physical pain in his chest as his heart fractured into even more pieces. "Sarah…but why?"

"Oh, why, he says! Why! Don't you remember what you said to me at the breakfast table before I decided to leave you on your own? Of course, you wouldn't remember, you never do with your vile fits of anger."

"Sarah, whatever I said, I swear to god I didn't mean it. You have no idea how unhappy I've been without you, how I prayed you were still alive."

"I don't care!"

"W-why not?"

"Because you said if I kept asking for children you would kill me!"

David couldn't believe it; this couldn't be real. "I said that?" he asked, the guilt as palpable as the lump in his throat.

Sarah broke down into tears. "Yes, you did!"

He couldn't help but break down crying, too. He wanted to embrace her, but she pushed him away.

"Get off of me! I'm just here to collect the rest of my things. At least Scott knows how to treat a woman!"

"Darling, please don't be that way, please don't leave – at least stay for a while. Have a rest upstairs. I understand why you want to leave me, I really do. I would, too. I've been speaking to a guy, this guy called Agent Carter, a tax collector, they took the Tempo, he's illuminated my behavior to me also, I just couldn't believe it when he was telling me."

"Good!" she yelled. "At least you aren't as stupid as I thought you were – the fact that you understand is better than nothing!"

"Sarah, please – take a rest upstairs in our bedroom, then you can leave me."

"Why?"

"I want to smell your scent on our sheets as a reminder of you when you're gone."

She glared at him, but for all it was worth, for the past twenty years they had been together, she felt she should allow him this final privilege. "Fine," she said, still livid, but calmer than she was before. "But that's the last thing I'll ever do for you!"

"Thank you…" said David, with a selfish kind of gratitude, knowing that he was the misogynistic pig Carter had made him out to be. He accepted it numbly.

The lifeless stillness turned into a storm of self-hatred as David sat on the couch again while Sarah was taking her rest. He sat there fuming at himself, cursing himself bitterly. The hours went by as he wound himself up like a thin metal wire, ready to snap and explode. Night turned into day without him realizing; he was too self-absorbed in his loathing. And suddenly…the bell rang. It was Carter.

David opened the door and Carter stepped inside without saying a word, floating past him like a ghost.

"Agent Carter," said David, his voice low and serious. "You won't believe what's happened."

"What happened, David? Did your goldfish die?"

"She's back!"

"She's back?" Carter furrowed his brows. "There's no car parked outside apart from my own."

"Wait – what?" David looked around to where Sarah had dropped her bag and keys. Her items were not there anymore. "No! She's here, I'm telling you. She's here! She's upstairs, sleeping!"

Deep down inside, Carter was overjoyed. Not for Sarah's return, but for what was about to unfold.

"David." He kept his voice low and firm. "There's no one here but you and me…"

David was utterly baffled. "What are you talking about?" he said, emanating an impotent anger. "She's upstairs!"

"Alright," said Carter coolly. "Let's go up and have a look, shall we?"

David hurried upstairs, Carter following him at a calmer pace. He ran into the bedroom, swinging open the door, and then he felt a sensation he had never felt before in his life. He was as puzzled as a newborn.

Sarah was not there. The bed was made, as he had left it. The room did not smell like her. He even looked for a loose strand of her hair on the pillows, her scent on the sheets. There was no sign that anyone had been in the room. There was no sign that anyone had come in or gone out of the house. If she had left in the middle of the night, he would have heard her; he'd been wide awake.

"Well? Where is she, my boy?"

"She was here! I swear she was here!"

Carter was ready to burst out in a fit of laughter, but he rammed it back inside him. "Oh, David…" he said, conjuring up as much fake concern as he could muster. "You – you've been hallucinating."

And the truth is, he had! There was no sign of her anywhere! He had made the whole story up in his head.

"And," said Carter, "no women were killed last night."

David felt an overwhelming compulsion to look at his hands. They felt wet and sticky; he could smell a pungent scent of iron in the air. And as he looked down, he couldn't believe his eyes – his hands were dripping with blood.

He pushed Carter out of the way and went to the master bathroom. He opened the tap and put his hands under the water, rubbed them with soap, but for all his efforts, he could not get rid of the bloodstains. He let out a tremendous scream of insanity. And then, he blacked out.

CHAPTER 7

Carter did not let him escape consciousness for long – he knew that was where David found his only relief from this nightmare of a life. He filled up a bucket with ice and water and tossed it onto David's unresponsive body. His feet twitched, his eyelids fluttered, he gasped and gulped in a huge breath of air and returned to consciousness against his will.

"W-what's going on?" he said, still blank from the abyss he had just returned from.

"Wake up, you psych-ward trash," said Carter, impatient.

"Jesus Christ, w-what's going on?"

Carter tossed him a towel. "Dry off, put some fresh clothes on and come downstairs."

It took a little while for David to find his bearings (if that was even possible at this point) and remember what had occurred. His life? A calamity. He dried himself off, put on a new set of clothes and went downstairs to find Carter, the unbearable pain inside him sharper than ever.

"Alright," said Carter as they sat opposite each other yet again. "You're going to tell me exactly what you heard and saw from start to finish."

"I – um – I heard her open the door." David's leg was restless, thumping up and down the whole time he spoke. "She came in, told me she was having an affair, said the reason was I threatened to kill her if she kept asking for kids. I complied. I only wanted her to sleep in our bed one last time so she could catch some rest and leave her scent behind on the pillows, something to remind me of her even though she had found someone else."

"She said you threatened to kill her?"

"Yeah."

"She wasn't real though, David, she was a manifestation of your guilt and fear. But inside this very fast-paced description of yours, we can – uh – come to certain conclusions."

"Like what?"

"Well, for one, even though she was only a hallucination, she was a part of your repressed psyche, communicating to you the truth about yourself. If what the hallucination of Sarah said about you threatening to kill her actually occurred in reality, and seeing her ghost in front of you was the only way to remember that – well, then, David, I would have to confirm my theory about you being a misogynistic swine."

"Great…" He hung his head in shame.

"David, this is really bad… You were in a completely altered state of mind. The fact that the hallucination of her told you that you threatened to kill her is an indication of what's happening in the deeper layers of your mind, or those blank spaces, as I like to call them."

"So – so, I killed her…and the blood on my hands…It wouldn't wash off."

"Now, what did I tell you about 'certainty,' David? *Stinks like the mouth of a whore.* Whenever you feel like you're certain about something, take a big step back, relax and think again, because nothing in this world is certain, my friend, and unfortunately for you, David, you're – uh – going to find that out. The really hard way."

"So now you're saying, even after that whole episode, we can't be sure it was me?"

"David, can I ask you a serious question?"

"Sure."

"Do you *want* it to be you? To be the one who killed her?"

"Why on earth would I want that?"

"Because then at least someone would shoulder the burden of responsibility for it for the rest of their lives and feel the overwhelming pain of the repercussion for their deeds – in other words, crucify yourself…instead of letting it be some insane, psychopathic bastard who does not give a damn."

"I could feel her – I could feel her pushing me back, pushing me away from her. I could hear her speak; it all seemed so real. Now I can't believe in anything. I can't believe in you either. I can feel you, I can press my arm against yours… but—"

"A mirage shimmering in the desert sand."

"This is the end. The end of me."

"Don't be pessimistic, David. Remember, there's still hope. Do you know the story of Pandora's box?"

"Yes."

"Well, then, cheer up and remember everything is going to be okay in the end, and if it's not, then it's not the end," said Carter, leaning over and giving David a little nudge on the shoulder.

"You – you can't be serious?" said David, furious. "You're taking a quote from Alcoholics Anonymous and planting it in my head after everything that I've just gone through?"

Now Carter really couldn't contain it; he started giggling again in mad delight. In between every gasp of air as he giggled like a fool. He asked for David's forgiveness, and David was just so broken, so desperate to be understood by someone that he let it slide, because Carter, according to him, understood him better than anyone else. He was his guru. So, it didn't matter what he said or did; there must be a good enough reason behind it, a lesson to be learned.

"Fine." David gave up, throwing up his hands. "Just tell me what I should do now."

"Now, you rest. You try to relax. This stress is driving you clinically insane, and the last place I want to see my old pal David is the psych ward."

"Alright, alright."

"Now, tell me, David: do you think it really was you that killed her, or do you *want* it to be you?"

"I'm - I'm not sure. If it were me, then I would wish death upon myself immediately. I would want to rot in hell for all of eternity."

"See, this opens up a new dimension to the puzzle," said Carter, raising his index finger in the air. "This has now become about the hidden relationship you have with yourself. And do you remember what I told you? We're here to find *you*, David. And once we've found you, Sarah will follow."

"Alright."

"You see, if we were to assume you are the killer, and we discovered her body buried somewhere in the backyard, and all you can say is that if it were you then you would wish death upon yourself...What would that make you?"

"A sick individual."

"Exactly. It would mean that not only did you kill Sarah because of your misogynistic tendencies, but you did it so you would ultimately get back at yourself. A sadomasochist."

"Right – right."

"How do you feel when you're shoveling plastic down that conveyor belt? Do you give yourself a healthy pat on the back after each day, or do you trudge through life, condemning yourself for the way things have turned out? Do you blame yourself for your miserable life, yet still return to it every day so you can't escape the pain?"

"I never looked at it that deeply. Must be another blank, I guess."

"Another blank," said Carter, growing increasingly satisfied about the position David was putting himself in, "and for every blank space in you, there is a jigsaw piece that fits. You've admitted it, David: *you hate yourself.*"

"Right, that's it!" said David, getting up and making his way to the backyard.

"Oh, what are you doing now?" muttered Carter.

David took a shovel and sank it into the grassy soil. Carter wasn't particularly bothered; for the first time, he actually may have felt sorry for him.

David spent about an hour digging holes in the garden, looking for Sarah's remains. Carter was watching MTV the whole time, until he heard a sob come from outside. David had fallen to his knees on the upturned earth, pleading, "Sarah! Sarah! Where are you darling? I'm so sorry...I'm so damn sorry!"

Carter opened the window that faced the backyard. "The hell are you doing, David? All you've managed to do is ruin a perfectly good yard. Now come back inside."

"Damn it," said David, panting. "You have no idea what I'm going through. I need Sarah, I need her back."

"The backyard is too obvious a place to look. That was merely an example, and if we think about where the body might actually be, considering how much you hate yourself, it's going to be a lot harder to find – because if you find her, well, the game's over; there is a telos, a conclusion, a line to be drawn. If you really did kill her, she wouldn't be in the backyard. You would want to make yourself suffer…She wouldn't even have a proper burial."

"Yeah, but since I hate her deep down, why would I want to give her one?"

"Humans are multifaceted, complicated creatures. When I call you a misogynist, you need to accept that, like it or not. There may be times when you feel an overwhelming sense of love for her, but that's a trick of the mind – the mind does that so it won't let you uncover the truth about your misogyny, because, in your eyes, you're perfect, aren't you, Davie boy?"

"I never said that."

"That's right, you never did say that, because that would be you admitting to your own narcissism, and that wouldn't make you perfect, would it?"

"But you said earlier I hate myself and that I'm a sadomasochist. How could I hate something that's perfect?"

"Because you're not perfect, and you know that, you just don't want to admit it, but you know alright, you know. There are many layers to the mind!"

"So, what do you think I should do? Give my life to Jesus?"

Carter scoffed. "Give his life to Jesus, he says. *After* committing homicide? How convenient. That's what Dahmer did, too. Commit the crime, repent and you are saved! Oh, please."

"So, I guess I should just hand myself in."

"Hand yourself in? You have no evidence you killed her and neither do they! Fool!"

"*So, what the devil do I do now, then?*" asked David, becoming increasingly frustrated.

"David, please don't talk like that. It would be best if you didn't conjure up *his* spirit, that's the last thing we need. Just… go upstairs, go to sleep for a while. I'll keep an eye on the news. Imagine Sarah is lying there next to you and you can hold her, tell her how sorry you are, tell her how much you love her. I think that would do you some good."

Carter knew holding on to the memory of Sarah, her phantom, so to speak, would do more harm to David than good. That's the only reason he was letting him go to sleep: it would make David long for her more.

David exhaled. "Alright. I'll try get some rest. I probably need it."

"Good man. Try to see if you can find any of her clothes from the washing basket – maybe you can get closer to her scent like that, just like you wanted to."

"Good idea. See you in a few hours."

MTV was doing a special about nostalgic moments in rock history. Carter was loving it, sitting there listening to "Gimme Shelter" by the Stones.

David, unaware of what Carter was doing, was facing his own form of nostalgia. He'd found one of Sarah's unwashed cardigans, and her smell, almost rose-scented, was sinking deep into his soul. He held on to it as if he was still holding her and spun her around a few times as if they were dancing lovingly. Then he took the cardigan, lay down in bed with it and disappeared into the abyss.

But not for long. For some reason, ever since Carter had come about, David had started to have dreams again. Sarah's scent was enough to bring back the memory of her. Of that raw honesty she held so close to her heart – there were no lies between them.

They were at the breakfast table again.

"David, honey?" she said gently, a huge contrast to the angry version of her he'd hallucinated. "Who's this man you've let into your house?"

David didn't really think about which man she was referring to, everything he said in this dream was a kneejerk reaction. "Carter? He's trying to help me find you. You have no idea how broken I am without you. Please, just come home."

"Yes, but isn't he a bit...*strange*? I mean, all he does is tell you all these horrible things...Are you sure you can trust him?"

"He's the only person I've got. I gotta trust him, he's a clever guy."

"Yes, but clever in what way? How does he make you feel?"

"How does he make me *feel*? I need to think about that for a moment. He...he makes me feel like...like *crying*."

"I don't think he has good intentions for you, honey."

"Oh Sarah, just come back, I've missed you so much."

"I've missed you, too. I still want to have children with you."

"Sarah – um – we...we don't have the financial security for that yet," he said, a slight hint of anger in his voice. Again, it was a kneejerk reaction; he couldn't filter his words.

Sarah frowned and looked down. Tears appeared in her eyes, then she slowly began to fade away.

"Sarah – no! Come back!" he cried in desperation.

He needed to be close to her. Every millisecond she faded out more, the closer he got to regaining consciousness, until finally he woke up, her cardigan soaked in tears.

Carter heard him moving around, so he quickly switched to the news channel. "You alright up there, pal?" he called out.

David came down the stairs slowly and steadily. He sat opposite Carter on the sofa and began describing what he had just experienced. "Saw Sarah again, in a dream this time though."

"Yes?"

"She wasn't angry, she was worried."

"Worried about what?"

"You," he said plainly, without too much hesitation.

"Me? In what way?"

"Well, she asked me if I think I can really trust you."

"Now, you listen to me, David, and you listen good. On a deeper level or on a subconscious level, we are all fragments of the one self. The one self being you. She was just a part of you, David. Or rather, what you know of her inside you."

"So, if I had seen you in my dream, who would I be talking to?"

"You would be talking to me, or rather, what you know about me that has just become a part of you."

"I see. So why was I – she – whatever, suspicious of you?"

"Well, only you know the answer to that, David. Are you suspicious of me? Do you think I want to hurt you? I'm sure it's felt like that…As I've told you before, I am shattering your illusions. But what? Would you rather I lied to you?"

"No, no—you're right. You're probably doing me more good than harm."

David had accepted that Agent Carter's true identity would remain unclear. He still didn't know who or what he was, but he was no longer interested in figuring out the truth. He had gone too far down the rabbit hole. Nothing could ever be "certain" again, and that's just what Carter had intended. Carter seemed to have the answers for everything, but they pointed David in no particular direction other than a slow dissolving of all boundaries.

To David's surprise, the doorbell rang.

"I'll get it," said Carter, in a tone that suggested he knew who it was.

In walked a slender man, about six feet tall, with dark hair that grayed on the sideburns and piercing blue eyes that looked at everything with sharp, transparent precision. He wore a nice, tailored suit with a crisp, white shirt and a slim, black tie. Intelligence permeated the man's aura – something about him reminded David of Agent Carter.

"Carter!" the man said in excitement. The two embraced.

"David," said Carter, returning to seriousness now. "This is Detective Hawke. Whilst you were sleeping, I was watching the news of course, and Sarah is still missing and hasn't been found yet. I called my old friend Detective Hawke to try to see if we can finish this damn puzzle."

Hawke's piercing eyes turned to David's confused face.

David sidled up to Carter and whispered in his ear. "He's not like you, is he?"

"What do you mean, like me?" said Carter, keeping his voice down to avoid embarrassment in front of his friend.

"He's not another figment of my imagination, is he?"

Carter brushed off the question completely. "Hawke, this is my old friend David. David, this is my old friend Hawke. We go way back."

David offered him an anxious and sweaty handshake. He could not know if the flesh he gripped was real or just another illusion.

"What's this old son of a gun Carter been telling you, huh, David? He's full of theories, isn't he? Oh, don't you worry, I've known him for quite some time now – I know all about him and the way he talks. Forget his theories if you want to remain sane.

"Do you want to know what my theory is about man? There are four fundamental principles: morality, prestige, power and grandeur. That's it. Do you see?"

"Um – I'm not quite sure I understand. What are you even doing here?" asked David.

"Well, Carter told me your wife has been missing for a while now. He also told me you and him weren't getting too close to any conclusive truth about the matter, so I'm here to help."

"He's here to help," echoed Carter, meaninglessly.

"What I usually do is test people based on my four principles before we begin, just so I can assess the situation a little better," said Hawke.

This was feeling all too familiar to David.

"So, I assume you're going to start asking me questions now?" said David. Little specks of light that looked like stars twinkled in his vision as he blinked neurotically. He felt the pressure.

"Let's start with morality," said Hawke, casually. "Do you believe you are a good person, David?"

David hesitated to answer. "According to what Carter and I have slowly been unraveling, I would say no. But it's not like we know for sure if I'm a good person or bad person – the truth is, with everything that's been happening, it's hard to tell."

"It's normal to be unsure, but think about the way you behave. You always try to do the right thing, don't you? Even when it's tough?"

"Y-yes, I suppose so."

Hawke smiled warmly. "That's your moral compass guiding you. Now, what about prestige? How have people viewed you in the past, how do they view you now, and how do you view yourself?"

"I've had a troubled past when it comes to my professional life. I used to work a government job, but people started spreading vicious rumors about me so I had to quit. Now I work at a plastic recycling facility. I feel less important. I feel like I'm a bit of a bum, actually, and I can't provide Sarah with the life she wants – pay is simply too low."

"I see, so your prestige is quite fragile. Well, not to worry, that's where grandeur comes in. In this sad little story of yours, you can flip your prestige around by believing you have a pivotal role to play in uncovering the mystery of your missing wife. Now, that is quite an important role, isn't it? So, don't worry about your prestige, you are a very important figure."

"I don't know – I just feel…lost," said David, the thought of Sarah twisting painfully in his chest.

"That's because you haven't fully embraced your power. You have the power to change things, change your life, find Sarah. But are you willing to take the first step?"

David looked up at Hawke with hope in his eyes. "I – I think so."

"Excellent," said Hawke, finishing his assessment. "Even though you are a complete loser and completely lost, I think there's still hope. I've been a detective for about fifteen years; I don't think it's going to be too much trouble to locate her."

The comment he threw at him about being a loser reminded David of how Carter toyed with him. He was still finding it difficult to accept that any of this was real, but after Hawke's assessment of the situation, David felt a small flicker of hope. If any of what was going on around him was real, then now was perhaps the time when the truth about Sarah would be revealed.

"Now, there's something you need to know," Hawke continued. "The women whose bodies were discovered at Stow Lake and then later in other areas nearby were mainly prostitutes. Therefore, the profile doesn't match when it comes to Sarah. The killer would probably not have gone after her – unless, of course, she was prostituting herself. Do you think she would have done something like that? Maybe to try to increase the amount of money you and her earned? If this is the case, then it would be a massive blow to your prestige, but please don't let that cloud your judgment. Try to be completely honest with me."

"Agent Carter," said David, in a low and serious tone, "get this man out of my house and out of my sight! How dare he say something like that about Sarah!"

"David—" Carter started, about to try to convince him it was alright, but he was cut off by Hawke.

"David, I am not trying to insult either you or Sarah. I am simply thinking objectively," said Hawke, as assuring as possible.

"Sarah never tells lies, she never hides anything from me. And she certainly wouldn't stoop to that level to try to recover our finances – she would get a job at a library or a clothing shop. But she's epileptic, that's the reason she can't work."

"You never told me that!" protested Carter.

"Well, I didn't think it mattered to you," said David.

Carter continued pressing him. "Now everything's changed! She may have gone outside, had a seizure and then died! Maybe she was a victim of her disease, not a killer!"

"Maybe…" said Hawke, contemplating the possibility.

David, through his own paranoid thinking, had neglected to consider the possibility she may have died due to an epileptic seizure. Now, it was as if a slight burden had been lifted. All the guilt and horror he'd wrapped himself in, convinced it was him who'd killed her, seemed to ease – but the pain of being without her was still sharp.

"Where did she tell you she was going the day she went missing, before you went to work?" asked Hawke, trying to probe for a solution.

David had to think really hard about this question. His memory problems got in the way of giving Hawke a definitive answer, but he dug into his mind and pulled out what he thought was the truth. "She said she was going into Cole Valley, as far as I can remember, to have a coffee and maybe look at a few clothes. But there is a possibility we had a heated argument that day about her wanting kids – and since I can't provide for them, well, it's possible she changed her mind."

"Cole Valley…" said Hawke. "Alright, we have a lead then. I'll go check out the area for any eyewitnesses."

Hawke shook Carter's hand, then David's sweaty one and left the house just as swiftly as he arrived.

Carter rounded on David. "You're a bloody embarrassment, do you know that?"

"Why?"

"This whole time we've been speculating it was either you or some lunatic who killed her. Now you tell me she has epilepsy, we can't be sure it's either. You damned fool. And how paranoid are you anyway? Didn't you ever stop and think that her disease is serious and could lead to a fatality? This whole time you've just been begging for it to be you. If you did it, would that help your *lack of power* a little? You pathetic worm."

"Well, Agent Carter, I'm sorry, it's probably just another one of those blanks."

"Blanks? *Blanks*? Screw you!"

"Alright, Agent Carter, I'm sorry…Would a cup of coffee make up for it?"

Carter was still only acting as if he cared. This revelation about Sarah having epilepsy didn't mean a thing to him. He brushed his hair back and massaged his head. "Two and a half sugars, and a biscuit."

"No problem," said David, happier now Agent Carter was apparently beginning to calm down.

They spent the rest of the time waiting for Hawke, drinking more coffee and watching the news station. Carter was clearly frustrated to not be watching MTV, but David didn't seem to notice.

Then, after a couple of hours, Hawke returned from Cole Valley.

"I asked everyone. I went to every coffee shop, every clothes store, the works – and no sign of her ever going there."

David sighed with a heavy heart, and Carter mimicked him.

"What about her medication?" asked Hawke.

"She takes Topomax," said David, trying to be of use.

"Yes, but when and how does she take it? Does she carry the bottle with her, or does she just take a pill and then leave it in the medicine cabinet?"

"She always just takes a pill before she goes out and leaves them at home."

"David," said Hawke, "check the medicine cabinet, see if her pills are still there."

David went to the master bathroom to check the medicine cabinet. Strangely enough, her pills were gone.

"They aren't there," he told Hawke.

"Alright," said Hawke. "If they aren't there, then we can presume that Sarah knew she was leaving the house for a prolonged period of time. It's time to find out how moral you truly are, David. Carter's told me a few things, but I want to hear it come out of your mouth. What's been going on between you and Sarah?"

"Well, like Carter's probably told you, we've been going through a sort of stagnant period in our marriage. As I said earlier, I don't have the money to provide for the children she wants, wages have gone down, and she's generally seemed a lot sadder for the past few months. I – um – hallucinated that she had come back and she told me she was having an affair with her doctor, her epilepsy doctor, come to think of it. Scott.

Carter told me my hallucination was a repressed memory, a repressed part of me type thing. I don't actually understand a word he says when he starts talking like a shrink."

"Well, he's well read," said Hawke. "I'll give him that. Do you have Scott's address?"

"Should be in the address book," said David. Carter did not interfere.

"I'm going to pay Scott a little visit," said Hawke, charmingly decisive. "Is it true that when you had this hallucination of her, she said you threatened to kill her if she asked for kids again? That's what Carter told me happened."

"It's true."

"Shame on you," said Hawke. "You should be disgusted with yourself."

"Well, it was a hallucination! How do we know that actually happened?" protested David.

Hawke ignored him. "Right, I shall see you after I have paid my little visit to Scott."

And that's how it was with Hawke: he was there for some time, then he disappeared again on the search for Sarah. David was feeling optimistic about this. He seemed to have someone on his side. Someone with skills and critical thinking – something he himself was not capable of. But he also never doubted Carter's usefulness. Carter had grown on him, become a person he couldn't shake.

Carter himself was annoyed that they had to spend the remaining hours of the day watching the boring old news channel, but just like nothing, a few hours went by and Hawke zipped back in, his search complete.

"Well, that didn't take long," said Hawke.

"What happened?" asked Carter as he yawned.

"She wasn't there either. David, does she have any other male friends you think she might have gone to?"

"No, sir. Scott's the only other guy I'll allow her to see."

"*Allow her to see*?" repeated Hawke. "What, is she your property or something? Is that what you treat her like?"

"Well, I – I don't want to lose her."

"See, that's where you messed up," said Hawke, the look of disgust fading from his face. "Putting terms and conditions like that on your marriage means she could practically be anywhere, or with anyone now – any other man that she knew and could offer her some relief from your pathetic ways."

"Well, at least we know one thing," said Carter, injecting himself into the conversation.

"What's that?" asked Hawke.

"He's certainly not the *moral* type."

"That's right," confirmed Hawke. He turned to David. "And don't think I haven't heard about your little meltdowns – you had Carter drive you to the police station so you could confess you were the killer. I'm starting to have a few *hunches* about you, David. If you know what I mean."

"This is unreal!" cried David, shocked at their attitude toward him.

"No, David," said Hawke, "what's unreal is how pathetic and impotent you are."

"Impotent?" David repeated. "Why did you choose that word? Impotent. Only Carter uses that word! That's it, I'm calling Chris!"

"Why?" asked Carter. "Hawke, Chris is Sarah's father by the way."

"Why do you want to call him?" asked Hawke.

David didn't reply to either of them. He flipped open his cell phone and dialed Chris. It took him a daunting thirty seconds to pick up this time.

"Chris, hi, it's me, David. I need to make sure of something. Can you talk to the two guys that are here with me right now?"

He passed the phone to Carter first.

"Yeah, hi Chris, good to hear from you again."

"Alright, pass the phone over to Hawke now," said David.

"Hello?" said Hawke to Chris. "Yes, I am a private detective that Agent Carter hired to try to locate your daughter."

"Alright, that's enough – now pass the phone back to me," said David. "Chris, did you hear their voices? You did? Alright, that's all I needed to know. I'll keep you updated on anything to do with Sarah. Stay strong. Goodbye."

"Why...did you do that?" asked Carter.

"To see if I'm the only person who can hear either of you. Both of you are freaking me out, making me think you're both figments of my imagination. Wouldn't be the first time that's happened – isn't that right, *Agent Carter*?"

"Well, how do you know you didn't just hallucinate the part where he told you he could hear us?" asked Carter cunningly.

"Damn you," said David. "To hell with you both."

"You know what I think, Carter?" said Hawke.

"What's that?"

"These are the words of a truly powerless man, with too much damn grandiosity. Delusions of grandeur."

"I agree," said Carter.

"What the hell?" said David. "What the hell are you guys trying to do, drive me insane? Power? Grandeur? What on earth are you guys even talking about?"

"*Twelve thousand dollars overdue*," said Carter.

"I would have to agree with that statement," said Hawke.

"W-what? Detective Hawke, what have you got to do with my taxes? See now, both of you are stepping over the line!"

"Do you know what a man does when he has a grandiose vision of himself but no actual power?" said Hawke, ignoring David's protests. "He seeks to find that power by any means he can. And I can only think of one power trip that would match the scale of your delusion. The ultimate power trip: To control whether a person lives or dies – in other words, to play God."

"I see...I see..." said David, defeated. "I killed my wife because I wanted to feel powerful – as powerful as God."

"He's got a god complex!" said Carter, who started giggling again.

"Carter, please – this is a serious matter," said Hawke. "We've now put David on the spot."

"Okay – okay, I'm sorry," said Carter, covering his mouth with both hands, trying to muffle the giggling.

"David," said Hawke, with a composure that made up for his partner's behavior, "this isn't the first time you've admitted to killing Sarah. You've done it before, but so far Carter has only managed to illuminate your potential motives – he hasn't gathered actual evidence. You see, with me it's a whole different ballgame. I am a trained detective, and I will figure out where she is, whether she's dead or alive, and finally, whether or not you are responsible for killing her. Do you understand?"

"Yes, Detective, I understand."

"Excellent. Agent Carter, it's time to go. And remember, David, I have eyes and ears everywhere."

They left David to battle out the uncertainty on his own.

David could not have predicted the accusations that came so quickly from Detective Hawke. There was a strange feeling inside him. He blamed himself for this, feeling like he was too weak of a man to fight back against these unknown men who'd come into his life. But there was also the feeling that they might know something more than he did, and that's what kept him clinging to them. He needed them, because he needed Sarah. No matter what accusations were made against him – that at times he'd been explosively angry with her, or too controlling – deep in his heart, soul and body, he knew that she was irreplaceable, the only woman he could ever love – and the love for her was deep.

In his impotent confusion, fear and anger, he started talking to himself.

"First it was Carter," he began, "with his psychobabble, psy-op bullcrap, now it's Hawke. Hawke! With his grandeur, morality and prestige bullcrap! They can't be real…How could they be real? How could anyone *normal* talk the way they do? No… No…I know what's going on – they're either feds or figments of my imagination. They're trying to drive me nuts! Unless I already am nuts! In which case, they only exist because I'm still alive! If I were dead and they were both part of my imagination, they would die, too! But they claim they can help find Sarah. That's the only reason I haven't ended this yet…We'll see…We'll see what we're *presented with* tomorrow when they come back…"

As he reflected on his words, he started laughing to himself like a maniac – he truly was entering a deranged state of mind.

A dangerous state of mind, even. And he laughed like that for hours, occasionally shouting out an insult to Carter or Hawke in between the laughter, until he tired himself out so much that he lay down and slipped into the all too familiar abyss. No dreams that night, though – nothing. *He was gone.*

CHAPTER 8

David's eyes shot wide open at around six-thirty in the morning. It was the sensation of being pulled back up to the surface from the deepest, darkest, least-explored ocean in the world. He panted. The first thing he did was look at his pajamas for any bloodstains, then he checked his hands and under his fingernails. Nothing. But the words of the police haunted him. They'd called the killer an "artist," and in the abyss, maybe he could discover some kind of hidden artistic talent in murdering innocent women. A familiar feeling of the uncanny crept back, fueling his paranoia.

He went downstairs and looked inside the food cabinets. Nothing but half a bowl of cornflakes and some milk that had expired that morning. Nonetheless, he helped himself to it – what else could this shell of a man do? He turned on the TV and switched to the news channel. For some reason unknown to him, it had been on MTV.

"Good morning, San Francisco," said the well-groomed anchorman. "If you're watching, you're just in time for the latest news on the killings that originated near Stow Lake then spread further out into the surrounding areas. Police have announced that a murder weapon has been found, but they refuse to provide any details on it, including details about DNA, due to complications in the process of finding the man responsible—"

Before the anchorman had time to continue with recounting the devastation these murders had caused, David turned off the TV. He chewed mindlessly through the small portion of cereal, the night before a blur to him, and simply accepted the fact that, in no time at all, Carter and Hawke would be ringing his bell.

Just as he had expected, the door rang at seven. But the all too familiar routine of Carter busting down his door and barging in to cause chaos was replaced by an even worse nightmare. Carter and Hawke were there alright, but not in the way he'd expected them to be. There was a police vehicle parked outside the house, and they were stood nearby. As he opened the door, they turned to face him, watching him with folded arms and scornful looks on their faces. But it was the police who had rung the bell.

David hunched over as they placed him inside the police vehicle. The fear of public humiliation scared him more than anything else – "the man who killed innocent women and possibly his own wife."

Carter and Hawke followed the police vehicle in their cars down to the station, where David knew he would be handcuffed, interviewed, then left to rot in a cell until the court case, where he'd already decided he would plead guilty to all charges. He would not even ask for a lawyer or plead the right to remain silent; he would confess outright that it was him.

It was the butch man, with the ponytail and the voice a tad bit too feminine for his masculine build, whom he found himself in the interrogation room with again.

"Well, well," the detective said to David, "here we are again. I did not expect this, if you want me to be one hundred per cent honest with you. Last time we met, you barely knew what was going on with you. I was genuinely concerned for your psychological well-being, but now it looks like your illness may have gotten the better of you."

"I watched the news…" said David, grinding his teeth. "The murder weapon…let me guess, my DNA was on it?"

"Detective Hawke is an excellent detective. He was the one who found it. The only problem is…things are slightly more complicated than we had foreseen. The fingerprints are only partial fingerprints. There are parts of the fingerprint which have a match to yours, but they could also belong to others with similar characteristics. The machine we ran them through said that there was no one definitive match, due to the 'incomplete,' if you will, nature of the evidence."

"What if I just admit to it, give myself in?"

"Agent Carter, a man who claims to have been observing you for a while, even going so far as to call you his friend, has told us about the unstable nature of your personality. We have three other men in custody whose fingerprints could match. These people are known criminals – one of them is, in fact, a known serial killer, who was released about ten years ago and could now be 'back in the game.' Like I said last time, David, yes, on one hand, you do not seem emotionally well, but on the other hand, there is overwhelming reason for me to believe that it *wasn't actually you*, based on the profiles of the other suspects. Now comes the trickiest question – why do you keep wanting to confess?"

"Because I can just *feel* it *inside* me. I haven't felt like this ever before."

"Based on that statement, we are going to have to keep you here for longer. We know the psychological profiles of the other men are terrible, but yours confuses us, and we need definitive answers. However, we have decided to accommodate you differently from the other suspects: we have allowed Agent Carter and Detective Hawke to be part of the interviewing process, as their insights into the way you think could be the key to solving this mystery."

The mention of Carter and Hawke made David's palms sweat. "Alright – alright, I understand."

Some of the other police who were monitoring the conversation via video feed in another room buzzed open the heavy metal door. Ponytail left the room and in came Hawke, ready to rip David to pieces.

"I told you," he began, "before I left last night, I have eyes and ears everywhere, and when I said that, it wasn't to try to make myself sound cool. It's not a grandeur thing, don't worry…It's the truth."

"Okay, and what do you mean by that…Detective?"

"It's a power thing. That's what I mean. We planted secret listening devices in your house and cameras outside at every angle to see whether or not you were leaving in the middle of the night. Thankfully, we didn't see you leave, but we did hear what you had to say about us and yourself – deranged…don't you think?"

"Well, I am very sorry – it's just that you and Agent Carter have been driving me insane."

"By doing what? Making some frank remarks about your character? Does that drive you insane, David? Knowing the truth about yourself?"

"How did you find the murder weapon?"

"See, unlike you, my grandeur isn't delusional – I have the power to back it up…Eyes and ears everywhere, pal. Golden Gate Park, that's where we found the weapon. I'm so well-known that I got an anonymous tip-off that there was some suspicious activity going on inside the park; someone who decided to bury something there in the middle of the night had been none the wiser that he was being watched. I brought a canine unit to detect any firearms or explosives. One of our dogs led us to the specific place in the park where the gun had been buried and, using a metal detector, we located it in the ground and dug it out. The weapon also matches the ballistics of the bullets found at the crime scenes. The deceased women were shot in the back of the head and hacked into pieces – we're still looking for the tool he used to do that. The point is, we, the police, are so close to putting you behind bars yet so far away, due to the nature of the evidence and the conflicting evidence with the other suspects."

"Right – right," said David, head hanging low.

"But you also know the profile of the women that were killed don't you, David? We talked about these women at your place. Prostitutes, most of them, and others were just promiscuous women. So, this is the part where I let Carter enter the discussion. I know how good he is at talking to you, discovering hidden truths about yourself and your personality."

Hawke looked up at the camera recording the session and beckoned for the cops watching to open the big metal door. Carter came in and sat down next to Hawke, who remained completely silent while Carter lay into David.

"You ever been with a prostitute, David?" was Carter's first question.

"I can't say I have."

"Do you think you'd have any reason to hate them?"

"I can't say I would."

"But you've admitted to me that you may have some misogynistic tendencies, do you remember that?"

"Yes, I remember, quite clearly actually."

"So, who's to say you don't hate women who exercise their sexual expression freely?"

"*I don't know.*"

"And what about Sarah, David? You said you would only let her approach one single man, her neurologist. Was that because you were afraid that Sarah might want to exercise her sexual expression freely?"

"Sarah would never cheat on me."

"How do you know she would never cheat on you? You admitted your marriage was failing, you kept her on a short leash – surely that would motivate her to want to be free of you. Wasn't it you who said that her *ghost*, the version of her you saw when you were hallucinating, told you that you said you'd kill her if she kept asking for kids?"

"Yes, but when I dreamt of her, she told me to be suspicious of you!"

"What about kids? Did she mention kids in that dream?"

"She did."

"And?"

"And, I let her down."

"You let her down. You see, *and she's still missing!* And it's because of you she's missing, isn't it, David? Now, I'm only going to ask you this one final time…Did you kill your wife, Sarah?"

David was overwhelmed. "I – I don't know! I swear I don't know! Why would I?" He banged his fists on the metal table and held his head down low, he was reduced to tears again. "Sarah! I'm so sorry, darling. Just come back…Please…please come back!"

"Alright – I think this interview is over!" yelled Carter. "Put him in the holding cell for twenty-four hours and we'll question him again tomorrow – we'll see if the claustrophobia of being inside those four walls won't *squeeze* the truth out of him."

They unshackled him and pushed him into the cell. The heavy door closed behind him. It had a single narrow window-pane for him to look out from – not that there was anything to be seen other than the blue silhouettes of cops walking back and forth – and a latched metal pane where they could pass him a plate of food or a coffee.

The walls were angry at him; they squeezed him tight as if they were about to crush him. A CCTV camera watched from the ceiling, monitoring the cell, except for the blind spot they allowed where the toilet was. It felt dehumanizing. He already felt reduced to an animal after the ordeal with Carter and Hawke – only then to be thrown into a brick-wall cage where his every move was monitored.

He craved the abyss, the blank space he went to, more than anything now, but there was a lot of noise. Other people who had been charged with crimes were going off inside their cells; the constant chattering of the police between themselves kept him awake, too. There was no option but to lie down on the plastic foam mattress, steel beneath that, which hurt his back, and try to slowly guide himself into the abyss, removing himself from his immediate surroundings, like being in a sensory deprivation tank, all with the power of his mind.

He shut everything out. The walls turned from something that suffocated into something that sheltered him from the outside world. He covered his ears with his hands to dampen the noises invading his head, and he closed his eyes, trying desperately, in this critical, stressful moment in his life, to drift off to sleep. To do so, he had to accept that he was nothing and that the world was nothing; he had to delude himself into believing that there was no meaning to what was going on in his life, that however cruel life was being to him at the moment, it was all just an illusion – a bad dream – and he wanted desperately to believe that he could escape from it, and when he finally found the courage to do that, he nodded off in the space of ten minutes and entered what he feared and loved the most... Nothingness.

But the police knew never to let someone sleep in their holding cell. They knew it was an escape, so about twenty-five minutes in, a policewoman violently opened the metal hatch and shouted, "Here's the coffee you asked for, David!"

David had never asked for coffee, but he was yanked out of the dark, yet comforting, territory he'd been hiding in and back to this nightmare with a bitter, crappy coffee in a Styrofoam cup. He was unaware of the time because none of the cell windows looked outside; all he had to go by was his internal clock, and the pendulum swung from consciousness into unconsciousness. One minute he was alert and frightened of being alone in the cell, the next he was wandering off inside the recesses of his mind, daydreaming. At least they couldn't take that from him, and he thought about his beautiful Sarah. He fantasized about her being found and his name being cleared, and giving her the happy life with the children she wanted, whatever it took to get there. Her warm embrace, her raw, honest love – her love for the world and nature, even though it was the design of nature that had given rise to her neurological disease. And then he came back to the holding cell again, snapping back out of the fantasy, his mind no longer free.

He stayed in that solitude for a moment, and his internal clock calculated that the next day had come and they would open the cell soon. For someone who was supposedly delusional, he was surprisingly accurate, because that's exactly what happened. Now he was ready for the next round of intrusive humiliation. He went unprepared.

Carter and Hawke were sitting side by side in the interrogation room. They handcuffed David and made him sit across from them, a cold metal table separating them. Hawke started talking first while Carter remained silent, just like the previous day.

"Listen, David, we're not here to play games anymore. We know about your erratic behavior and your warped mind; we know that you've confessed it was you multiple times. Just tell us how it is we find a partial fingerprint that matches not only with your prints but with those of two other felons, one of them being a known serial killer. You seem to think we've been messing with you this whole time, isn't that right? But the evidence tells us otherwise. The evidence proves that someone is messing with us right now, messing with the law. Is that you, David? Did you plant the evidence there on purpose? Are you doing all this for attention? To feed your grandiosity? Does it make you feel powerful, knowing that we're all scrambling to find the truth – trying to save you from yourself? Trying to find your wife?"

"I wouldn't know the first thing about planting fake evidence, let alone have access to the murder weapon that's responsible for killing those girls."

"Well, it's not that difficult – all it would take is a quick internet search. Touch the gun, smear the print with a cloth, and allow the environment – heat or moisture – to distort the print even further."

"This is crazy! I don't know anything about planting false evidence!"

"Let me get at him," interjected Carter. "What about your memory lapses? Could you have done it during one of those times? Try to reach into the darkness of your mind, try to remember."

Hawke removed the gun from a sealed bag and placed it on the table. "Does this refresh your memory?"

"I swear, I've never seen or handled a gun like that before in my life."

As things became less and less certain in the interviewing room, there was a sudden commotion outside. The big metal door buzzed open and Ponytail came rushing in.

"The other suspect," he said, trying to catch a breath. "He's bitten down on a cyanide capsule he had hidden in his mouth. I'm talking about the ex-serial killer."

"Jesus Christ!" said Carter, furious. "Take me to him, now!"

Ponytail guided him to the other interrogation room where the ex-serial killer was slumped sideways on the chair, froth escaping from the cavity of his mouth. He probably had a very short time left to live. Carter quickly opened his briefcase, where he had a picture of Sarah. He showed it to him.

"Did you kill this woman, you sick bastard? Talk!"

The man was unable to speak, but he stared at the picture with the intensity of the dying, fear blaring out of his eyes, and subtly shook his head from side to side. He had never seen her before – or at least, that's how Carter interpreted it. Then he passed from this realm to the next, leaving a trail of questions behind him. Did he kill those girls down by Stow Lake? Did he kill Sarah, or was her death completely unrelated to those other girls?

The game had changed. Carter charged back into the interrogation room where David was being held.

"Looks like you've had your lucky break," said Carter. "He took himself out before we could put him away for good. His actions prove that he was behind the killings; he just didn't want to spend the rest of his life rotting in jail."

"And what about Sarah? Did he kill her, too?" asked David, shaken by what had just occurred.

"The look on his face when I showed him her photograph… He didn't seem to know who she was."

"So, that leaves us with one conclusion." Hawke jumped in. "The killings of the girls down by the lake and the fact that Sarah is still missing are two completely unrelated incidents."

"So, where is she?" asked David, desperately.

"That's it, let him out of here," said Carter to Ponytail. "He doesn't have a clue and neither do we. There's no evidence to prove he killed her – nothing's shown up yet. All I can say is I don't know who's more sick in the mind, you, David, or the guy who just killed himself."

"We can't just stop looking for her!" cried David.

"No one said that was the case," said Hawke calmly. "The path is narrower now – things might actually start getting clearer."

A cop came into the interrogation room and unshackled David. They escorted him back to his home in one of their vehicles. Carter and Hawke's presence lurked inside David on the ride home. He knew they weren't done with him yet. But as far as the law was concerned, there wasn't enough evidence to prove that he had killed Sarah, despite his many confessions, which could not be taken seriously as they were from a man who was believed to be paranoid and out of touch with reality, probably due to the stress of his wife's absence. Ponytail told Carter and Hawke that he wanted to put David in some kind of psychiatric setting, maybe an asylum, but they argued heavily against it, claiming that they were in control of him and that they would help him find his clarity.

They arrived at David's house more or less the same time he did, letting themselves in.

Hawke took a look around, located the address book and held it up in the air. "Right, David, I am going to be gone for a long time now, searching for Sarah in every single address in this here book. Once I've found her, you will reimburse me for my efforts, but don't worry, you can pay me back in small instalments monthly. For the traveling expenses, I mean."

With that, he was gone, and David was sure he would not return for a very long time. The list of people in that address book was huge and Hawke would have to travel to different states to visit them all.

Carter seemed in his own world, his mind elsewhere. "Hmm. *Twelve thousand dollars overdue.* What do you think about that?" he said, flashing David a sarcastic smile.

"Don't you think it's time we left the tax thing behind us?"

"As you wish, but to be honest, I would tell Hawke not to bother – he's not going to find her anywhere in that address book."

"And how do you know that? Right now, Hawke is the only thing I have left. He's my lifeline."

"He never actually cared about you, or Sarah."

"What? What are you talking about? He's on his way, probably to five or six other states, to find her."

"How can you be so sure of that? Maybe he's decided to go on holiday and have you pay for the expenses."

"Why would that be the case, after everything we've been through together?"

"*Twelve thousand dollars overdue.*"

"Oh, come on, Agent Carter. Please stop messing with my mind."

"Now that you mention your mind – how do you feel? Do you still think I'm a figment of your imagination? A federal officer? Or do you think I'm your old pal Agent Carter the tax man?"

"After our interaction with the police, I'm pretty sure you're real."

"And you're sure about that, are you?"

"Yes."

"Good. That's good for me."

"Why? You've been desperately trying to convince me otherwise."

"You'll find out in time."

"Again with the riddles and the uncertainty."

"You know how much I hate certainty."

"Why do you hate it so much?"

"For all the reasons you love it."

"Right. And what reasons would they be, then?"

"Certainty breeds stagnation, lack of creativity and growth. Think about your stagnant marriage – all you do with Sarah is come home from work, eat some frozen food, then stare at the TV like vegetables until it's time for bed. She's tolerated that for so long because of you – and then you wonder why she's gone. Certainty makes you close-minded. How can you be innovative and think more broadly if you're certain about something? Life is inherently uncertain – you know that better than anyone, probably more so than anyone I've ever met. It's not just the fact that Sarah's gone missing, it's that you've been bouncing all over the walls trying to figure things out in that pea-sized little brain of yours, to no avail. I value uncertainty because I value the unknown; I find it far more exciting to explore new worlds. You just want your little job, your crappy little house and your obedient little wife, don't you, David?"

"So, you think Sarah's gone because I've made her complicit in a life she doesn't want?"

"There you go again, trying to find certainty in a situation that has no certain answer. You bore me, David, do you know that?"

"Well *excuse me* for trying to find answers to where my missing wife is!"

"Hawke's on the case."

"You just said he wasn't!"

"I wasn't talking from a place of certainty. I was just talking, speculating – I like speculation."

"So, how can I trust anything that comes out of your mouth?"

"Look, David, I'm just a *guide*, okay? I make speculations about things, that's what I do. It's up to you whether or not you want to believe them."

CHAPTER 9

David now understood a critical aspect of Carter. He had talked about certainty before, but David had been too confused to
really grasp how Carter thought. David knew that it was his
own unfortunate mental impotence that made him fall easy
victim to the web of illusions Carter spun while claiming he
was dissolving David's own. He was now fiercely alert.

He thought back to the time when he had slept with Sarah's
cardigan, her rose-like scent somehow creating clarity in him.
It was the power of her love.

He wanted Carter out, and he was certain of it this time.

"Well, guess what, pal?" he said. "I don't need a *guide*, I
need the *truth*. And as far as I'm concerned, I don't think you
actually know the damned truth, do you? All you've ever done
is get a rise out of me. And I've had it with you. So, get out of
my sight or I'll call the police."

"You'll be surprised about how much truth I actually know.
And unfortunately for you, I'm not going anywhere. If you try
to call the police, I'll call Hawke, and I'll tell him not to look
for Sarah, and he'll do exactly as I say. You seem to forget who's
calling the shots here, buddy."

"Calling the shots? So, now I'm your captive?"

"David, David, relax. You're not the first person to become
upset after I start ranting about certainty. I think you're too on
edge right now, and it's probably my fault. Look, we can wipe
the slate clean, can't we? Forgive each other. Move forward
onto a more enlightened path."

"What would you possibly need to forgive me for? I haven't
done anything to you!"

"Well, you have."

"What have I done to you?"

"Every second I spend with someone of your caliber is an insult to my image of myself."

"Sounds a bit like the *delusions of grandeur* Hawke accused me of having!"

"Please, David – unlike you, I'm fully in touch with reality."

"Really? And how do I know that, coming from a man who says he's not certain of anything?"

"No, David, you're the one who's not certain of anything. I simply use uncertainty as a tool to consider every possible scenario."

"I see. So, you're saying it's better not to know anything because then you know everything?" David understood the paradox in what he was trying to say, and it impressed him slightly.

Carter was weaving the web again, so David began to calm down.

"That's it, now you're starting to understand. Come on, David, sit down next to me, don't put the news on, stop searching for the answers and relax. Let's put some MTV on and have a breather from the tension. I know Sarah's fine where she is – I can feel it. She'll come back, maybe Hawke will find her, who knows? Uncertainty is liberation. Trust me."

David complied with Carter's wishes. They switched the channel to MTV just in time to hear the song "Because You Loved Me" by Céline Dion. For David, this song obviously reminded him of Sarah, only heightening his need to find her. But for Carter, this song reminded him, without the implication of any erotic attraction, of his bond with David in an ironic way – and he was loving it. He genuinely believed in the emotions the song evoked, that he was David's savior, but with that black twist of irony he infected everything with.

"Come on, David!" he yelled above the music. "Sing the lyrics with me!"

David began to feel the inappropriate connection Carter had found in the song and sat there in silence, feeling the kettle of anger start to boil up again. He knew how to deal with this. He had formulated a strategy. Instead of engaging with Carter, he would sit there and stare blankly into the void, saying and doing nothing, until Carter got so bored that he would have no option but to leave David alone.

"What's the matter, David – don't you like Céline Dion?" Nothing. Not a word. He stared blankly in the other direction, ignoring Carter completely.

Carter caught on to David's trick pretty quickly and admired his attempt. But this just gave Carter the opportunity to play a different game. He turned off the TV. He could smell the fear coming from David, and as always, this amused him.

"What's going on, Dave? Why aren't you saying anything? What are you staring into space for? Is there something wrong?"

No response. Carter waved his hand back and forth in David's vision. His eyes did not move.

"Ah, I see, another form of mental breakdown. You've become catatonic. Do you know what, David, the ponytail cop said he wanted to put you on meds. You know how well-read I am about certain subjects – I'm actually quite well-read about pharmacology, too. Have you ever heard of a drug called olanzapine? Its brand name is Zyprexa. It's an antipsychotic medication. We could put you on that. And once you get better again, you can become an affiliate of the company that produces it. The face of recovery. You can go around telling people how much good it's done for you and they can pay you for it. Maybe that could provide some extra income – you know, for the children you want to have with Sarah!" He started to giggle manically again, knowing how badly he was getting on David's nerves, which showed when David dropped the act. The kettle was steaming.

David jerked around quickly to get a grip on Carter's neck, but Carter, much younger, much stronger and well-built, fought him off.

"That's it," said Carter with satisfaction. "Get angry! Get angry! I like it when you get angry, David!"

David knew it was useless to put up a fight. Carter was getting a buzz out of it as well, which made him stop wrestling with him.

"Damn you, Carter! Just leave me alone!" he said, his eyes glazed over with tears again.

"That's it, David. How do you feel right now?"

"You just get off on my pain!"

"Well, I won't abandon you as easily as you think. Playing dead won't work either, and I caught on to that game pretty quickly, which is something you should give me credit for. Come on, David. I'm trying to help you!"

"How are you trying to help me? You have no empathy for me!"

"This situation doesn't require empathy. It requires a cold, calculating mind."

"But Agent Carter, Hawke's the one who's gone looking – you can't expect me to sit here beside you watching MTV until he gets back. Please, I'm begging you, give me some time to be alone with my thoughts. That's the only place where she exists right now. Sarah, I mean."

"Okay, David. I understand. You're right. I haven't been the best of companions. Maybe you need a break. Spend some time in your thoughts, where you can be with her presence. I promise, when I come back, I'll have a little bit more of that empathy you're asking for."

"Alright, thank you for understanding."

"Hey, hey, David. I've understood you since the moment I set foot through your front door the first day we met. Don't worry about it. I'll be back in a few days, maybe a bit longer. Hey, listen – just call me when you need me."

"Alright, thank you. Goodbye, Agent Carter."

When Carter shut the door behind him, David felt his anger and confusion turn into relief. Amazingly, Carter had suddenly turned into a better man. For what may have been the first time, he'd showed a little bit of understanding of what David was going through. A weird turn of events, and David wasn't sure how long it would hold up for. But at least there was now some distance between them.

He sat in absolute stillness, taking the lesson he had learned from being in the holding cell at the police station and applying it to the situation he was in right now. He was still helpless and alone; his only hope was that Hawke may discover Sarah at a distant relative's house in another part of the country. But in the holding cell, he had learned how to shut off the outside world, he had learned how to make the pendulum swing and enter a compartment of his mind where Sarah's memory was still alive. The more he approached her as just a mere memory, the more he feared that her physical presence in the real world would fade, so sometimes, he held back. But when he found the courage to go there, despite how fleeting memories actually are, it was almost like finding love again for the first time.

He thought about what Carter had told him, about when he was actually dreaming about her, not just sitting in a trance: that she was a part of him, and everything he knew about her was what was speaking to him. So, he found her in that way in his mind, and, not knowing how long the trance would last and when she would slip away again, he talked to her.

"Sarah, I can feel you here with me. We're looking for you, honey. I promise we're going to find you."

"Hi, David. How have you been without me? I'm sorry I've gone missing. But it's not my fault."

"Darling, just tell me what I did wrong. Tell me why you felt unhappy."

"I just felt like we're getting older, and now was the right time to start a family. But because of the situation you're in… we can't have one."

"Darling, I promise, if you come back, we'll have a family."

"Tell that to the real me, if you ever find her."

"Tell me straight, Sarah – did I do anything to harm you?"

"Only the real me can ever know that. I'm just her memory."

"It doesn't matter if you're only her memory, I still want to be close to you. This is the only place where I can find you."

"I love you, David."

"I love you, too, sweetheart."

"Go to visit Stow Lake. It's safe there now, the police have cleaned the area up. Maybe you'll find the answers to where I am there. You know how much I like being outdoors in nature. Go to Stow Lake."

"But I want to stay here with you forever. Even if you're just a memory. What am I going to find at Stow Lake? It's been stained with the blood of innocent women."

"I can't stay here with you much longer," said Sarah, fading away as David began to slip from his trance. "Just do as I tell you. There may be some answers there."

"Don't leave me! Please! I need you!"

He lost his grip on her presence, and found himself alone. He felt like breaking down into tears. He was unsure how many days it had taken him to get into the state of mind where he could find and talk to her, only to spend a dishearteningly short time together. But she had left him with the idea to go to the lake. Maybe she was right, even though she was just an avatar of Sarah he had created; maybe her presence knew something he didn't.

The bus there was for poor people who couldn't afford to own a car. Some held their belongings in plastic bags. Though the bus was nearly empty, the stagnant heaviness of the few other passengers reminded David of himself. He got off at a stop nearby and walked the rest of the way to the lake. After the serial killer's suicide, the cops had cleared up the yellow tape. But that meant nothing; it wasn't ever going to be the same lake he had gone to whenever he wanted to be alone with himself. Now he was alone with the corpses they had found there, even though they were long cleared away.

He sat on the bench, everything around him still, except for himself and his racing mind. He was trying to find what Sarah had told him in a whirlwind of thoughts. A violent paranoia grabbed him and suddenly hauled him back to those thoughts and feelings of having been the one responsible for her death. The lake could still be keeping secrets from him, is what he thought, secrets that only existed in the abyss.

Was this what she wanted him to feel? The threat of his own identity? The identity of a madman?

He stood up from the bench, unable to take the violent storm of his emotions anymore. The world around him spun; the lake went from a blue-brownish hue to a vile blood-red.

He ran all the way back to the bus stop and stayed there to re-collect the fragmented thoughts, which still raced and still churned with guilt and fear. He waited too long for his liking; he needed to get back home. His impulsivity was taking over again, the impulsivity Carter had warned him about, or maybe even planted in him – he couldn't tell the difference anymore. But he was intent now, after fearing that he could still be responsible, on entering the abyss forever.

He was trembling when he entered his home, his mind resolute. He went up to his bedroom and opened the wardrobe. This was where he kept his double barrel. He picked it up. Its heftiness, the texture of the wood grip, the cold iron of the barrel all seemed to cry out to him, offering him the final solution, calming him with the promise of the end of his suffering. His vision went a hazy red, everything a blur, as he put the barrel in his mouth. His finger was barely able to reach the trigger, but if he stretched himself enough – well, that would be his demise.

Then came the hope from Pandora's box. He remembered what Sarah had told him before he went to the lake, her soothing, loving voice. *"I love you, David."*

His vision stabilized, the fear of death, of maybe leaving her behind in this world, wherever she was, if she was still here, returning to him.

Carter was right: he should never be certain about anything. He shouldn't have let the paranoia take over, driving him to be certain, yet again, that he was the one responsible. And when the thought of Carter came into his mind, his words echoed inside him, too, his words about calling him if he had any need for him. So, David decided the best thing to do was to call him, to use him the same way he perceived Hawke: as a lifeline.

"Hey, David!" said Carter, sounding very cheerful. He'd taken no time at all to pick up. "Didn't expect you to call me so soon, how are you?"

David was choking on his saliva and his tears. "Agent Carter – I – I just tried to kill myself…"

"Jesus, I should have known better than to leave you to your own devices. It's only been three days, and look at what's happened. I'll be right over if you need me to. Stay on the line."

"How long will it take you?" asked David, out of desperation.

"Ten minutes. I'll be hasty for you, old friend."

"Alright, just stay on the line."

He could hear the noise of Carter fumbling around to get in his car. "Alright, I'll stay on the line for you, pal. Don't worry, I'm coming."

"Thank you."

"So, what made you do this?"

"I went to the lake, couldn't handle it, started thinking I'm responsible for Sarah."

"And what stopped you and made you call me?"

"Sarah – and you, that thing you said about never being certain. I figured I might be making a mistake. I'm banking on Hawke finding her, alive."

"Good choice. It would have been a shame to lose you prematurely."

"What do you mean?"

"I mean, too soon – before Sarah comes back."

"Okay, how close are you?"

"I'll be there in five."

"Alright, I – I think it's okay if I close the phone now. I'll be downstairs waiting for you."

"Alright, David, see you in five."

"See you."

David put the gun carefully back in its place and went downstairs to make Carter a coffee. It was the least he could offer him. He could sense that Carter hadn't been lying to him; he'd sounded way more understanding, a lot more empathic. David had left the front door open, and exactly as he finished making Carter his coffee, Carter came inside. He looked at what David was doing and could smell the aroma of the coffee in the air.

"Back to your senses so soon?"

"Barely. But I feel better. Here's your coffee – thanks for picking up the phone."

"Uh – your emotions, David. They're – uh – labile. You switch from one state to the next very quickly, is what I'm trying to say."

"Yeah, *I know*. It's kind of always been this way, just less intense. You have no idea how much stress I'm under, no idea how much I miss her."

"Well, it's alright. Hopefully, my company will keep you stable – unless you want me to call the ponytail cop, maybe get you on some medication?"

"I don't want any. I know they've all got terrible side-effects. I just need some stability, that's all. And some hope."

"You sure? If you become the face of recovery and strike a deal with one of these pharma companies, you could be rolling in it! Ah, just kidding! Gotcha!"

David began to see Carter in a new light, a better one; he was being truthful when he'd said he would return a different person. David even laughed at Carter's joke. "My old pal, Agent Carter, the tax man," he said.

Carter patted him on the shoulder. "I'm glad you didn't do it. Honestly, I'm here for you."

"I'm glad I didn't either, Agent Carter – imagine if we find her, then what would have happened?"

"You don't need to call me 'Agent' anymore, David, just call me Carter. And yes, you are correct. And I am sure we will find her."

"Do you really think there's hope?"

"Wasn't it hope that saved your life?"

"Yes."

"So, there is hope."

David opened his arms and embraced Carter, thanking him for his kind words and help in this troubled time.

Carter patted him on the back firmly. "It'll be alright," he said. "I promise."

Rays of gentle white light filled the room as the clouds parted in the sky. David was sure, now, that this man was on his side. And Carter was sure that this would later work in his favor.

As David pulled away from the embrace, he looked at Carter directly in the eyes. There was something there, something of the old Carter, that cold, calculating glare, but it soon shifted into an undeniable warmth, giving David the grounding he deserved after so long in starvation for the truth.

Carter could see what David felt, but could he *feel* it himself? That's the question David should have asked himself, but he didn't. Then, Carter invited him into more conversation.

"Shall we sit down together?" he suggested, prompting them to sit in the familiar old living room.

The tension was slowly easing its way out of David. He made a satisfied groaning sound, letting go of some stress, breathing in the aroma of freshly brewed coffee, finally comfortable with Carter being there.

Carter noticed. He took a sip of his coffee. "Things are dark right now, I can understand that. But you have more strength inside you than you think. Believe me. Let's talk about Sarah, what are some of the good times you two shared?"

All it took was Carter's mention of her for her to haunt him again; he was still desperate for her to return, but he put those feelings aside for the time being.

"We used to go to Stow Lake on the weekends," he said, wishing he could forget the lake and the power it had over him. "She used to bring bread with her to feed the ducks. She loved it when they would make those quacking sounds and flutter their wings at her feet. It isn't easy to forget how grateful and happy she was for moments like those. Moments that the average person – myself included – would overlook. She always had the most innocent soul. An innocence that could never be mine."

"David, you sound bitter about yourself. I want you to remember that you are a good person. That memory sounds beautiful – can you think of anything else about her?"

"All these years, I took her for granted. I can remember more about me than I can about her. I can remember how jealous I used to get, even in the better days when I had a bit more cash to spare, taking her out. She used to wear her pretty dresses and her cardigans; other men would look at her, talk to her. I just kept all that rage I felt when I got jealous inside, and some days I wasn't able to keep it bottled up anymore. A beautiful girl like her, having to deal with my jealous ranting, my insecurities. There were times when I could say I put her through hell. That's why I'm so scared of myself, scared about what I might be capable of. I'm still scared, Carter…I'm still feeling pain, regret, loss, confusion. You understand me better now though, don't you?"

"You've got to learn how to forgive yourself, David. And we've been through all the possibilities of what might have happened to her – it's useless to keep talking about it, you're just digging your own grave. Don't forget, Hawke is your ally. He's on the case."

David's phone buzzed in his pocket. He went from covering his face with his hands, hunched over, to reading a text message from Hawke: *"I'm still looking, David. Don't lose hope. We'll find her."*

Carter leaned over and read the message, too.

"That was no coincidence," he said. "You need to start trusting the universe. If Hawke says we'll find her, he's not fooling around – it means he's looking, high and low."

"He's removed the listening devices from my house, right?"

"Of course, David. Try not to be paranoid."

"I'm sorry, it's just that…you've changed so quickly. I don't know why you care about me all of a sudden. Don't worry, I'm glad you're on my side, I guess…my paranoia just peaks at certain times."

"Try not to listen to it, David. I have always cared about you. It's just, at the beginning, I needed to use a different tactic to show you that; I needed to break down your ego. Now that's not necessary anymore."

"I understand," said David, but it was his impotence talking.

"So, no hard feelings, right, David?"

"Right…" David's voice trailed off, his mind elsewhere.

"What are you thinking about, David?"

"You're not going to believe this. You don't understand how much of a jackass I really am."

"Don't feel ashamed, just spit it out. I'm listening."

"I cheated on her, Carter," David blurted out. "Back when we got married. Just before that, actually. I wanted my last chance to feel like a free man. I was young back then, better looking, stronger, more sociable. I was attractive to a lot of women. One night, I went out, told her I was going to see a friend, might not come home until the next day. I went out looking for another woman, my final taste of unmarried life. This woman knew her; Sarah found out. It broke her heart. But she still stuck with me, out of her relentless love and loyalty. And she still agreed to marry me.

"I don't deserve her. I never deserved her. I'm making an oath right now...If she comes back, I'll find a higher paying job – I'll look everywhere – and give her the family she wants, the life she wants. I need her more than ever, I need her warmth, and I promise to give her some of mine – as much as there is in me, even though I doubt there's much. But I'll find it when she comes back. I promise."

"Hey, we all make mistakes, David. There are much worse men out there than you. Sex offenders, drug addicts, gamblers, rapists. You're not like them – it was a mistake, that's all. I'm sure, when we find her, and you get your soul back, things will be better than ever."

"I hope so..." he said, still trapped in thought.

"David, how about we do something to get you out of this slump? Remember the first time I walked in your door, you said something like 'hell, why don't we just go fishing!' I still remember that remark, even though what you were really saying was you didn't want me in your house anymore. Well – why don't we try going fishing? We can pick up a six-pack from the liquor store and just let go for a while. We'll be in nature – that'll remind you of some positive memories with Sarah. You'll loosen up a little bit, we can carry on talking. Come on! It'll be fun!"

"I'm not going back to Stow Lake," he said miserably. "I hate that place, I hate what it's done to my mind."

"That's not a problem. We can drive southwest to Lake Merced!"

"Isn't that a bit far?" he said, looking for an excuse not to go.

"Only fifteen to twenty minutes, depending on traffic. It's not far at all. Come on, David! What's the matter with you?"

Carter's excitement rubbed off on him. "Oh, alright. Fine. We'll go fishing."

CHAPTER 10

"I've got the rods and reels in the back of the trunk already!" said Carter, slapping the trunk of his car. "We'll go lure fishing, try to catch us some nice bass! There's rainbow trout down there, too. Did you know that?"

"You brought the gear with you?"

"Yeah, I had a good feeling we might head out somewhere nice today – and trust me when I say that I knew we weren't going to Stow. No way. I know how you think, David! Don't forget that!"

Carter knew David like the back of his hand. That should have made David wary, but this new, friendly Carter had thrown him off.

Carter had a tape player in his car. He popped in a Led Zeppelin album and the song "Stairway to Heaven" came on. Carter drummed his fingers on the steering wheel and sang along. David found it suffocating and rolled the window down.

"Can you turn this song off, please?" he asked, as politely as possible. "I don't like it, it's not something I want to listen to right now."

"Gotcha," said Carter, perked up about the fishing trip. "I understand. Did you know that in the eighties they figured out that if you play this song in reverse there could be satanic messages in it? I don't believe in that bullcrap, it's all a bunch of rumors and conspiracy theories. But I do believe in subliminal messages, that's got to have some truth to it."

"I don't really care too much for conspiracies, you already know that. Plus, I'd rather not talk about it. Makes me uncomfortable."

"You're right, David. We'll just turn the music off and I'll roll my window down, too. I like the breeze flowing in, feels good."

As the breeze swept into the car, the tension seemed to subside. David breathed out slowly, the cool air soothing the heat behind his eyes. Carter's presence still felt like the lifeline he needed, strangely enough.

As they drove toward Lake Merced, the cityscape of San Francisco transformed into stretches of green land and blue skies. Worry and fear somehow faded into the background. But David wasn't fully able to let go of the weight of everything that had happened – the disappearance of Sarah, the guilt he carried, the horrifying uncertainty. However, there was something about this moment, sitting with Carter beside him, driving toward a new place, that made him feel that, somehow, he may just be able to breathe again.

"Alright, here we are!" said Carter, pulling into a small parking lot near the lake.

The lake gleamed in the afternoon light, its glassy surface reflecting the clear blue sky above. There were a few fishermen scattered along the shore, and the soft sound of water lapping at the bank created a feeling of much-needed tranquility.

David got out of the car. Carter was full of enthusiasm, already pulling the fishing gear from the trunk.

"You ready for some bass, my friend?" he asked in a playful tone.

David forced a smile. He wasn't sure if this fishing business would really help him clear his mind. He didn't want to disappoint Carter, though – this was his way of trying to help, and David couldn't deny the small feeling of comfort that came from it.

"We'll see how it goes," muttered David, taking his rod.

The gravel beneath their shoes crunched softly as they made their way toward the edge of the lake and found a good spot near the water. Carter set up his tackle box and cast his line quickly and efficiently. David's movements, on the other hand, were unsure and awkward.

"Have you ever been fishing before?" asked Carter, watching David fumble around with the reel.

"Once or twice. But that was years ago, don't remember too much about it."

"Don't worry about it." Carter tossed his line into the water with a satisfying swish. "Just focus on the present moment. The past and future should not be your concern right now."

David watched Carter's movements, the rhythm of them oddly calming. It was as though Carter was trying to help him get in touch with how simple the world was again – away from the mental anguish that consumed him.

For a long time, neither man spoke. The only sound they could hear was the gentle splash of the bait hitting the water. A calmness settled into David's mind, a brief relief from the storm.

"This is nice," he said after a long time, his voice gentle, like the water. "I'd forgotten what it was like just to experience… some quiet."

Carter nodded, scanning the water with his eyes, his expression unreadable. "It's easy to forget, David, you know, when life gets loud, and we forget how to just listen to the world around us."

David wandered in his thoughts, the rhythmic pull of the fishing line grounding him in the present. He thought about Sarah again, but when he saw her face, it wasn't the terrifying image of the missing person poster or the nightmare of her disappearance. He was close to her now—close to the Sarah from the past. He could recall her laughter and the way her eyes gleamed when she looked at him, the way they were happy before everything went wrong.

"I messed everything up," said David quietly. "I took her for granted."

"David…" Carter's voice was soft. "Stop punishing yourself. You made a mistake, yes. But the past can't change. All you have is now, right now. And you have the chance to make things right – the power to change is in this moment."

David didn't reply right away. He stared at the water, watching the ripples spread from his baited hook. Although he wasn't sure he could change things, Carter's words had settled deep inside him, shifting a part of his mindset.

For what felt like hours, they sat in silence. In the sky, the sun was slowly sinking lower. David hadn't felt this kind of peace in ages. He couldn't help but think that maybe he could change – maybe Carter was right, maybe he could correct the flaws in his personality, maybe he could make things with Sarah right again.

Carter was the one who eventually broke the silence. "So, do you want to tell me more about what's been eating at you? I've been listening to you, but I'm not just here to throw you pieces of advice, I don't want to come across as pretentious. I want to hear it from you…What's really going on in your mind?"

David's mind drifted once again, back to the moment in his house where he nearly pulled the trigger. His deep desperation had been terrifying to him then, but now, sitting by the calm waters with Carter, it seemed a distant memory, an aspect of himself he no longer wanted. He was unsure if he was ready to face the full weight of what he had almost done, but Carter really did feel like the old friend he kept saying he was, and this made him feel like he was rising – slowly and carefully, but rising nonetheless.

"I almost took my life…" said David, the pain in his voice so tangible. "We need to find Sarah. I have to make things right, and I swear to you, Carter, I'll try my best."

"That's all I need to hear, David. I promise you we'll find her." Just as he said that, a bass bit the bait on Carter's hook, and excitement took over as he reeled it in. "You see, David! In the same way we're casting our lines out there, never knowing when we'll catch some nice bass, Hawke is out there, working tirelessly for you on the case. He's throwing his line out too, in unknown territory, and I promise, just like we caught this one, we'll get your Sarah back!"

With a triumphant grin, Carter reeled in the struggling fish. Its silver scales shone under the fading sun as it flopped on the grass. Carter held it up proudly, like a trophy, and David couldn't help but smile – even though it was half-hearted; his mind still busy with thoughts about locating Sarah.

"Well done, Carter," said David, summoning up as much happiness as he could. "You always know how to turn everything into a metaphor."

Carter chuckled, unhooking the fish and placing it in the cooler. "Well, it's a bloody good one, isn't it? Think about it – Hawke's out there digging, chasing every lead, every scrap of information. He's exactly like us, casting his line in and hoping someone bites. But he won't stop until he gets there. You finally have the chance to feel optimistic, for once."

David's gaze returned to the water, the slow motion of the ripples a comforting and simple sight. But he was still a swirl of emotions on the inside. *Hope, effort, trust* – these were the feelings that Carter's words conjured up. Every thread wove together into one simple picture: finding Sarah.

"You really believe we'll find her, don't you, Carter?"

Carter softened his expression. His taunting cruelty had relinquished itself, replaced with something that felt genuine. "I've got to, David, you've been through hell. You *are* in hell right now, but I'm not going to let you go through it alone. And as for Sarah…we're going to find her. I'm telling you. You aren't going to face this alone, not while I'm around."

Carter's conviction was contagious. David didn't know if everything would go back to normal, if they would find her – but for the first time in days he felt like he could breathe, and even though this was a small thing, just a small breath of air, it was enough to remind him that maybe there was still hope.

"You're right, Carter." David's voice was still quiet. "Maybe this is the right time to start trusting the people who are trying to help me. I've drowned in guilt and fear for too long."

"Exactly!" Carter's voice was full of energy. "You just have to keep going. It's all about action – you made the right move calling me when you needed to, letting me back into your life. Trust the process, trust your team, trust the universe."

While staring out into the fading sunlight, David let his fishing line settle in the water again. Shadows stretched long over the lake, but the warmth of the day hadn't faded out just yet. Although not entirely free from worry, he felt lighter. *Keep going*, were Carter's words, and they stuck with him. It was all he could do now.

"Alright, Carter." David's eyes met his friend's. "I'll keep going."

Carter widened his grin. He slapped David on the back. "That's the spirit! Now, let's catch us some tasty dinner. But don't get your hopes up too high – I'll be the one catching all the fish today."

David did what he hadn't for a while: he laughed. A full, hearty laugh he couldn't help but let out. It sounded strange, even to him, but it was something good.

Looking down at his rod, waiting for a bite, his thoughts still circled Sarah. He tried to stop himself from getting too optimistic, but for the first time in forever, he thought maybe – just maybe – they were getting closer. Closer to the truth. Closer to her.

The line suddenly went taut and pulled, jerking David out of his thoughts. He set the hook and began to reel it in.

Carter shot him a look of surprise. "Well, look here! Catching our own fish now, are we? Looks like David's on board!"

With his full attention on the fight between him and the fish, David did not respond. It wasn't just because of the catch, there was a sense of determination, something he hadn't felt since Sarah's disappearance. His heart was pounding, and with a final tough pull, David reeled in the fish. It wasn't as big as Carter's, but it was his small taste of victory, which felt good. Really good.

"There you go," said Carter proudly. "Not too bad, see? Sometimes it's about finding the right place to cast your line."

"I guess so. Maybe I just haven't let myself see that there's more to life than misery and confusion."

"Exactly!" said Carter, giving him another slap on the back. "We'll find Sarah, and when we do, it'll be better than you can imagine. Trust the process, you're on the right track. Trust me, trust Hawke – that's the kind of attitude we need to move forward."

Just like all the possibilities, the lake stretched before him, calm and vast. David felt something inside him shift. Carter was still examining the fish David had reeled in.

"This might be a female fish, David. I have a good idea – how about we name it Sarah and let it go free back into the lake, where she can find her home?"

"Good idea, Carter."

"Here," said Carter, handing him the fish. "You set her free. There won't be much for dinner, but that's a small loss compared to the magnitude of what this moment represents."

Gently and with love, David released the fish back into the water. It flopped its tail around until it was fully submerged, then swam freely in its natural habitat, feeling the joy of being there, under the clear waters again, where it would live the rest of its life unharmed.

Carter cleaned up the fishing gear as the last of the sunlight bled into the horizon. Their fishing expedition had come to an end. Carter was very satisfied, and David, he just felt that tad bit safer inside his own mind. They took a comfortable journey back to David's place, put the frying pan on high heat and seared the bass nicely, the kitchen filling up with the aroma of a healthy, warm dish.

As they took their seats at the dining table, Carter had a little surprise for David. He reached into his jacket pocket and pulled out a small bottle of whiskey. "Care for a taste?" he asked, his light-hearted playful spirit still there as he unscrewed the cap and poured a hefty amount into David's glass.

David thought about it for a few seconds. Nothing was tempting about it – he was always careful with alcohol and felt that he wasn't in the right mental place to drink – so he pushed the glass toward Carter. "Not for me, brother. I don't think I can handle that stuff tonight."

"Suit yourself." Carter picked up the glass and knocked the whole thing back in one big gulp. "You see, the reason I pulled out this *elixir*, if you will, is because I wanted you to relax completely, to numb down your feelings a little. You see, I think about it this way... When I *feel things* for too long, it starts stressing me out. I don't particularly like the idea of 'feelings,' if you get my gist. And you, well you're in the eye of the storm, you're caught in a whirlwind of emotions. I hate seeing you go through that."

"I understand what you mean, but I witnessed firsthand what alcohol does to a man. Remember when we talked about my father?"

Carter had completely put that behind him, but something jerked in his memory. "Oh yeah, your dad. Sorry, I completely forgot. I hope my drinking doesn't come across as insensitive?"

"No, it's fine. Each to their own, I guess."

"Right, thank you," said Carter, pouring another heavy glass. "I think it's time I confessed something to you. Ever since I met you, us two getting close and all, I've been drinking a little heavier than I normally do. It's just that your situation is really heavy, and all of us have our way of cooling down. You see, I'm an educated man – self-educated actually, as you know – and I also know a lot of things about culture. Life is violent, man. Life is heavy. And getting *too close* to a person like you, in the situation you're in – I never liked it. It made me angry, actually."

David stopped to process what Carter was telling him for a moment. It was as if the mood had suddenly changed.

"I – I guess I understand what you're saying. Look, Carter, I'm sorry if my case has caused you to lose any sleep. I know it's disturbing. I know that firsthand – it's hell on earth for me, man. You said it yourself. But didn't you say we were looking forward toward the best? That Hawke is going to find her?"

Carter took another sip from his glass. His fingers traced the rim, slowly and smoothly, almost as if he were savoring the weight of David's words. The smile on his face wasn't too wide, it wasn't too forced – it was the kind of smile that made David feel like everything was still okay, that his feet were still on solid ground.

"Yes, I said that, didn't I?" was Carter's eventual response, in a low and steady voice. He tipped his head slightly to one side and leaned back on his chair. "And when I said that, I meant it. Hawke is a good person. He's got the skills he needs to find her. He will find her. But the thing is, David..." His pause stretched just long enough to add tension. "The thing is, we're in this together, you and me. And you're carrying all that weight on your shoulders alone, I can see it. I want you to get through this. But I want you to be *ready* when we find her."

For a moment, David was quiet. He was trying to understand what Carter was really saying. It sounded soothing to some degree, yes – but there was a subtle undercurrent he couldn't quite make sense of.

"Carter, I get it. But carrying this with me is not something you need to keep doing. I can face this on my own. You've helped enough already."

"Oh, I know, I know. But David, sometimes...sometimes, even once you're past the point where you can do everything by yourself, you don't realize how much you need other people. Do you understand what I'm trying to say?"

David thought about it for a while. It sounded like the kind of thing that makes people feel better, the kind of thing friends tell each other. But something was tugging in the back of his mind – something that felt like Sarah. It lingered, a distant memory he couldn't quite grasp.

"Well...I guess so," murmured David, his voice sounding a little strained. "You know, it's just I can't see things the way you see things – see them clearly, I mean. I've been living in a fog for too long."

With a soft clink, and with his eyes fixed on David, Carter put down his glass. It felt like it was almost too much to meet the intensity of his gaze. David found himself with his nerves back on edge, fidgeting. It wasn't anything too overt – nothing about it screamed manipulation – but there was something about Carter's quiet attention that made David feel like he was going to pull more from him than he could really give.

"David, when you're stuck in the fog, sometimes you don't see things clearly. You're stopping yourself from moving forward, even though you think you're protecting yourself."

Carter's voice drew David in. "It's what's keeping you stuck... You've got to let go of that fear."

David felt the gravity of what Carter was saying. His chest tightened under the weight of his words, without him knowing why, because he didn't quite understand what Carter was trying to tell him.

"I'm doing my best to let go," David quietly replied, his eyes dropping to the glass on the table. The honey-colored whiskey glimmered in the dim light, and he couldn't help but imagine what it would be like just to taste a little, to free himself of everything. But as quickly as it came, the thought faded. He shoved it down. He couldn't afford to do that.

Carter swirled the whiskey as he picked up his glass again and took another sip. As he drank, his eyes never left David's face. David felt like there was something he wasn't seeing, something beneath Carter's calm exterior. But Carter broke the silence before he could realize what.

"David, look," he said, leaning forward a little, his voice casual but with an edge that couldn't be ignored. "We all struggle. We all carry our burdens. And sometimes, yeah, the weight of it all feels like it's crushing us. But ask yourself: are you going to allow yourself to be crushed? Or are you going to fight through it?"

David didn't respond immediately. His mind spun again. He was caught between the warmth of the whiskey and Carter's words, which caused a subtle shift in the atmosphere, a tension that built with each lingering question.

"I don't know – I don't know if I can fight through it anymore," said David, finally.

Carter gave a little smile at that, but it wasn't the same smile he had given earlier. This one was tighter, more knowing. "You'll find a way," he said, softly, almost as if he was speaking to himself. "You always do. Don't you, David?"

Without knowing why, David felt that sentence stick with him. Something about it felt off.

Carter gulped the whiskey, setting his glass down with a sense of finality. He gave a smile to David, but it was a smile that felt too reassuring, too perfect, as if everything had already been decided, everything under his control.

"You'll see, David. Soon, things will turn around. Just keep that head of yours on straight. Don't allow those *feelings* to control you." Carter's voice still sounded reassuring, but something about it felt like a warning.

David swallowed, trying to digest both the food and the words placed before him. He nodded, grateful for Carter's help, but some tiny thread was telling him he wasn't seeing the whole picture. He just couldn't figure it out on his own.

"Thanks, Carter," he said, more out of habit rather than anything else.

Carter's tight grin widened. "Anytime, David. Anytime."

In that moment, the shadows in the room loomed a little taller, the kitchen light dimmed a little more. David didn't understand what had changed, but, for just a second, he felt like he was losing control.

Carter didn't seem to notice – or maybe he did. Either way, he kept his mouth shut.

The plates were pushed aside, the meal was finished, and they were left in a weird, unsettling silence. Carter stood up from the table, and as though he had just won a small victory, he stretched with exaggerated satisfaction.

"Alright, let's move to the living room, David." He grinned as he scooped up his whiskey bottle and glass. "Time to relax a bit more; you deserve it."

David didn't protest, although he was physically worn out, numb, despite not having touched a drop of alcohol. The house felt quiet, and they shuffled into the living room, where Carter slumped into the old couch and turned on the TV. He flipped to the local news channel. David sank into the armchair beside Carter, his thoughts still on Sarah, fingers shaking.

The anchor was a woman this time, and she gave a quick, practiced smile as she began to talk. "Good evening, San Francisco. The city has recently been plagued by an epidemic of reckless driving, with five accidents occurring in the same day and law enforcement agencies saying they are going to crack down on distracted and drunk driving. We'll have more to say about that after the break. And now, in sports news…"

David's chest constricted, his breath shallow. He blinked a few times in disbelief, hoping that the next segment would be about Sarah. But nothing came on. There was a report about a drunk man crashing into a tree and then a report on a local high school basketball team. His hopelessness sank in deeper and his stomach turned. The city and the world had moved on. There was no mention of Sarah, no updates about her story. Everyone had forgotten her; the news didn't care anymore and neither did the world. All she was now was a statistic, left behind like bones thrown to a blind dog.

CHAPTER 11

"So, David. How do you feel?" asked Carter, in a tone that was almost too relaxed.

"I – I don't get it. The news didn't even mention her. Nothing. The world's just forgotten about her."

Carter made an understanding face and nodded thoughtfully. But it was like he was savoring a secret; it seemed too slow, too self-absorbed. "Yeah, you're right, I guess. But hey, don't take it personally. That's just the way things are, right? People move on, they forget. That can't be changed."

The words swirled in David's mind as he stared at Carter. Even though a part of him already knew, he didn't want to believe it. The world *was* moving on, leaving her behind. It crushed David, it suffocated him.

He gripped the armrests, like he was trying to hold on to something real. "I don't know how I can do this! I don't know how I can move on! How do I let go…of something like *this*?"

Carter's eyes were unfocused. He leaned back in his chair, contemplating something far greater than the confines of the room they were in. When his voice came, it was soft and steady – measured, almost – like he was sharing a secret that only a few people could understand or accept. "You know something, David – some people are just wired differently. Everyone's got their own philosophy, their own way of perceiving the world. Some people *want* to find meaning in everything. But there are a select few of us that don't need meaning. We don't have to *fix* things. We accept that things are random, chaotic and unpredictable. And that's just the way it is, the way life is supposed to be."

David was unsure whether Carter was speaking to him or just lost in his own thoughts.

Carter continued, with a distant gaze and a sharp voice –
but there seemed to be no malice in it, just a detached sense
of clarity. "Some people go through their whole lives trying
to impose meaning on things. They'll search for answers
in things that just haven't got any. They'll look at suffering,
death, loss and think *why*? And they'll spend their whole
damned lives running in circles searching for a crumb of
meaning to answer any of those questions. But here's what
I think – sometimes, there's just no answer. It's all random,
David. And by trying to force meaning from it, well, it's like
trying to catch water with a net. Completely futile and exhausting. And eventually, it will break you down. You just
end up holding a net with nothing in it, wondering...what
the hell did I do wrong?"

Carter's words pressed against David like an unbearable
weight. How could he accept randomness and meaninglessness when it hurt him so much? It made him want to push
back, it made him feel unsettled. If what Carter was saying
was true, then what did that mean for Sarah?

But Carter was already leaning forward, not giving time
for David to respond, as if he was trying to pull David deeper
into his ideas. "See, some people – well, most people, actually
– they desperately want things to *make sense*. But they're going after something that doesn't exist. Illusions. That's all they
are. People who cling to justice, fate or God – whatever it may
be – they hold on to these ideas because they need to believe
in something. But what if it's all just a game? What if every
tragedy, every triumph, everything that actually happens to
us is just an outcome of thousands of tiny random little vari-
ables no one has control over?"

The conversation had stretched on for too long. David
sank into his chair, closing his eyes, pain, regret and shame
weighing on him heavily. Both men fell completely silent for a
few hours, and Carter watched David drift off into the abyss,
knowing full well what emotions were inside him.

It was exactly three in the morning when David was fully
asleep.

Carter got up, patted him on the shoulder and said, "Good luck, buddy. You're definitely going to need it."

He shut the front door behind him and disappeared into the night, leaving his words to do their work in David's subconscious.

Days passed. David tried reaching out to Carter a few times on the day after their conversation. Then, once again the next evening. The phone calls went unanswered. Carter was just busy, was what he told himself at first. But doubt crept in as the silence stretched on.

It felt intentional to David. Perhaps it was a test. Or Carter just didn't care anymore. David felt as though Carter thought he could just pick him up and set him down at a whim, as if David was just one of his many projects.

Every time he checked his phone, his frustration grew. No texts, no missed calls, nothing. Not a word from Carter.

David was becoming increasingly anxious. He stared at Carter's number as he paced up and down in his living room. As if it held some kind of answer. Then he would call, just once, thinking surely Carter would answer. But the call went straight to voicemail each time.

Late one night, he was sitting on the couch, the dim flickering of the TV glowing against his gaunt face as he flipped through channels aimlessly. It was a device to keep his mind occupied, but it was a poor distraction. The news droned on, flashing out new stories – robberies on the other side of the city, politics on the other side of the world. No mention of Sarah.

His heart was racing. He tried calling Carter again, but there was still no answer. Then he tried Hawke. Silence again, the call going straight to voicemail.

He was terrified. The silence made him feel smaller than he could imagine; it was suffocating him. He needed something, anything, to pull him back from the edge. He needed to hear Carter's voice.

His memory took him back to the fishing trip, when Carter had felt like a beacon of hope. This silence, from both Carter and Hawke – it robbed him of that beacon.

Was Carter purposely avoiding him? Had he had enough? Was the weight of the situation too much, even for Carter, who always seemed so confident and so *together*? Carter's words had given him a sense of purpose, a strange comfort, despite how unsettling they were at times. His confusion and pain had become somehow *manageable* in the grand scheme of things when Carter was around to talk to him. Carter had provided him with a sense of direction, however distorted.

The truth was, David relied on Carter. Now, with Carter's silence, his sense of stability was evaporating.

David stared at the blank screen of his phone as he sat on the edge of the couch. He wasn't able to breathe. There he was, in a spiral of worry and regret, as the outside world moved on. How could he survive without Carter's words? David was in a raw state of panic.

It was almost as if he had gone into a state of withdrawal. At this point, he hadn't heard from Carter for a week. The words Carter had left him behind with were stained in his mind. His philosophy: *Randomness, chaos, meaninglessness.* David obsessed over it. He couldn't escape the idea that things were beyond his control. He drowned in his impotent helplessness. Carter's philosophy was cold and brutal, but David felt that it *did* explain things. Maybe no one actually *owed* him an answer, or anything else for that matter.

His thoughts turned into a slow-burning despair. The silence began to feel like a noise, and it was deafening him. Every unanswered call brought him one step closer to the abyss.

Finally, late in the evening, David's phone rang. His heart palpitated; his breath caught in his lungs. Anticipation made him feel like he was about to collapse. He answered on the first ring, not even looking at the screen, shoving the phone to his ear.

"Carter?" he said, his voice like a tightrope, stretched to its breaking point.

"It's me, yeah," came Carter's voice, casually and smoothly. He sounded at ease, not bothered by the intensity between them. "You've been calling for a while now."

David's grip on his phone tightened, his stomach in pain. "I've been trying to reach you for days. Where the hell have you been? What the hell is going on?"

Carter exhaled slowly and with measure. There was a long pause before he talked again. There was a slight clinking of a glass in the background, as if Carter was sipping on something. Probably whiskey. David felt like they were in two separate worlds entirely. He felt isolated.

Carter's tone remained neutral, without a sign of guilt. "I got your calls, man. I got your messages. I – uh – am sure you were worried. Look I just needed some time to think about all this, about *you.*"

"Carter, please. I just need you to explain. I need to know why you've been so distant. What's been going on? And why isn't Hawke answering either?"

There was another long pause from Carter, and when he spoke again, his voice was infused with a hint of something that sounded like...frustration? David found it hard to place.

"David, it's not you, alright? It's the whole situation. You're dealing with your own crap, and I get it, I really do get it. But I can't be around that sort of thing all the time. As for Hawke, I've spoken to him, he's still out there working for you but he's working slightly slower than he anticipated. This case is a spider's web, or at least that's how he described it to me. But what I want to put the most emphasis on is that this is emotionally draining for me. I never wanted to get *this close.*"

David's confusion deepened. "I have no idea what you mean. What are you talking about?"

"It's not easy being around you, man. You've been messed up since I met you, tangled up in this mess. Listening to you talking about Sarah for so long just...eats away at me. You're in pain, I get that, that's no surprise. But you *cling* to it, David. And you've been leaning on me for every little thing."

"I don't understand. I thought we were friends. Carter, I need you. I need someone like you to support me – I'm dying inside, man. She's not even on the news anymore! The only people I have around me to help me are you and Hawke. Please stand by me."

There was another long pause. Then Carter spoke, barely changing his tone, but there was a trace of something sharp in his words. "Listen, I don't want you to worry about Hawke, but let's get back to me for a moment. It's not like I don't want to be around to help you. But I can't carry you…that's the thing. Carrying all that weight for you, all the time." There was an almost clinical detachment to his words. "You need to find a coping mechanism, a way to deal with it yourself. You've got to realize that you're not the only one going through hard times right now. Life won't stop just for you."

David wanted to respond, but Carter kept going, like he was reading off a script.

"It's not your fault, man," continued Carter. David felt like he was a child being talked down to. "You're in a tough spot, and I understand. But watching someone sink into that kind of hole…It's not easy. It's exhausting to me, you know? Being around someone who *expects* you to pull them out."

"So, what? You're just going to give up on me?"

"No." Carter's reply was instant. But in that single word there was something cold, something that didn't come from a place of compassion. "I'm not going to give up on you, David. I just want to give you space to figure this out on your own. Toughen you up a little bit. I can't be the one holding your hand through all of this. I've got work…I've got my own life. What can I say. I'm sorry."

Carter's tone went light and casual again as he continued inflicting a mix of hurt and disbelief into David's chest. "Man, I don't know. You need to understand something…Empathy doesn't work like you think it does. You can't always *feel* someone else's emotions. I feel like I'm being dragged into it. I have to stay above it now, do you understand? I can't be dragged down into the mud with you every time. Not anymore."

David couldn't bear to hear this. His mind raced. He was unable to process what Carter was saying, but somehow, his words made sense. Carter was not lying. Not exactly. And he never sugar-coated what he said. But something didn't feel quite right, like Carter was hiding something important, like there was a layer to this conversation that David didn't have any understanding of.

It was Carter, the way he spoke. Controlled and distant, like he wasn't touched by the emotions of the situation one bit. And with that thought came a tiny spark of realization in David's brain: Carter didn't really care about setting boundaries. The plain fact was that there was no *real* care behind his actions. There wasn't any *real* empathy. There wasn't any compassion. It was all just words designed to make David feel that the only cure to his helplessness was Carter.

But that spark in his mind was just too small. David couldn't actually see through Carter's game. He just *couldn't*.

"I understand," he muttered after a prolonged silence. "I – I think I understand you, Carter, don't worry. You're right…I need to stop bothering you. I have to figure this out on my own. Just promise me one thing."

"What's that?"

"That Hawke won't give up, too."

Carter went quiet for a moment, then gave an empty, humorless chuckle. "He's not going to give up on you. I won't allow that. And I'm sure you'll work things out. You've got to – I can't do it for you anymore, I'm afraid. Learn how to cope."

The line went dead.

The call had ended on a bitter note. David was buried under six feet of soil. There was only one thing he could do now: try to get into that trancelike state where he could talk to the avatar of Sarah in his mind. That's how alone he truly was, talking to a memory of a person who he was still worried might be dead. But he had no other choice. Unless, of course, Carter cooled down at some point and came back – which was likely, because Carter was unpredictable like that – but for the time being, the avatar of Sarah was all he had left.

First, David walked to the window and stared out at the city lights. Out there, everything was happening. Life. While he was stuck in this void, the world kept turning. He felt completely alone, his breath was shallow, he was trying to silence the storm in his head, to step out from the unbearable reality of his life. To the place where he could talk to her, where her voice sounded real.

The ritual began. His breaths were deep and slow, his muscles relaxing. His mind needed to be clear from all distractions. But that wasn't easy – not anymore. Like the distance between two people in a dream, the space between him and the physical Sarah had grown. Carter's haunting words still echoed in his head. The harder he reached out to her memory, the farther she slipped away. But he couldn't stop now. He had to try.

One breath at a time, he let the tension drain from his body. His pulse began to slow down, but it wasn't the same as before. The more he tried to force his way into the place in his heart where she resided, the more his heart forced him back out. His doubts and his anger kept intruding in his head. His mind was rebelling against him.

But he kept trying. He breathed. In. Out. In. Out. Like the soft tide of an ocean. The space between his breaths felt endless. His thoughts faded out, replaced by a painful longing. He exhaled shakily, terrified yet relieved. She was there. He could feel her.

"Sarah," he whispered inside himself. "Sarah, can you hear me?"

The echo of her, the phantom in the recesses of his mind, replied. "I'm here, David." Her voice was soft and steady, as if she had been waiting for him for a long time. "I'll always be in here."

"I need you. You have no idea how much I miss you. I feel so…lost without you. I need to know if you're still out there and that you're okay. Are you okay?"

She didn't answer immediately, and when she did, her words were like smoke in the air. "No, David, I'm – I'm not okay. But I'm not really gone either."

David fought hard to stay with her. "I don't know how to survive without you. I can't keep going on like this. I need you. Where are you? What do you mean?"

"I can't come back, David." Something about the way she spoke made her words feel final. Like a door closing.

"I can't let go. I can't do it. I don't know how."

"For your own sake, David, you have to. It's hurting us both, it's hurting you more than it hurts me. You can't hold on to this forever. Let go of me."

"I don't know if I can…"

"You will. I believe in you. You'll find your way." Her voice was so soft, yet so final.

"Where the hell are you?" he broke out angrily, shattering into pieces.

"I can't tell you. I'm just the memory of Sarah. But I live in your heart, and I know that the tax man you've let into your life…he's no good."

"Explain."

"I'm sorry, David, I can't stay with you any longer. I have to fade away again now."

"Please! Sarah! I love you. Please don't go, please don't leave me here all on my own." His eyes were closed and he was deep in the trance, but there were tears streaming down his face.

With that, her presence faded. She slipped away like sand through his fingers. Her image, those large, glowing, beautiful eyes, gone. Leaving him with the despair of silence, her absence breaking his heart. He was alone.

***

Carter didn't come back immediately. As the weeks stretched on, David was crippled by loneliness. Sarah's words about *the tax man* made him doubt everything again – his sense of reality, his ability to cope on his own. The words continued to echo in his mind, gnawing at him. He couldn't ignore them, but he tried to force them out, praying that Hawke was doing the right thing. Praying that she would come back.

Then, as if some universal power was testing David, the phone rang again. The number flashed on his cell phone and he hesitated. It was Carter.

His gut began to churn; he felt sick. Was Carter calling to help him? Or to try and make things worse? The seconds ticked by like an eternity before he pushed himself to answer the call.

"Carter?" said David, his wounds cracking through his voice.

"David." Carter sounded the same as usual – cool and unaffected, like it wasn't the first time they'd spoken in weeks. As if he was stepping in from a long day, mimicking David's simplicity. "It's been a while, man. How are you holding up?"

David's stomach twisted. He had been trapped in his thoughts for so long, isolated, stuck with Sarah's memory. Carter's voice felt like an intrusion. Something wasn't right.

"I – I don't know how I'm *holding up.*" David's voice faltered. "Where the hell have you been, anyway? You just disappeared! Do you have any idea how bad it gets when you leave? Why haven't you called?"

Carter's voice came back slow, still too calm. "I was, uh, drinking a little," he admitted, a small chuckle escaping from him. "Listen, I was probably talking crap last time, man. I didn't mean to leave you hanging. You've felt low, and I just didn't know what to say – you know how it goes, right? But I shouldn't have just disappeared on you. You're right. I made a mistake."

As Sarah's words played back in his mind, David's heart raced. *The tax man, he's no good, he's not your friend.*

He tried to sound more certain than he felt, even though his voice was trembling. "Carter, I – I don't know. I've thought about things, and I don't know if you're being honest with me or not. I feel that by trusting you when I shouldn't – I've been lying to myself. Is this all *something else,* or are you genuinely trying to help?"

There was an unsettling lack of vulnerability in Carter's voice when he replied. "David…" he began slowly, weighing each word. "I understand. You're in pain. But I can't be your babysitter. I can't constantly drag you up from the hole you're in. You can't keep pushing this on me, otherwise you're going to push me away, for good this time."

This again. Like a switch had been flipped, the blame falling on David, his words feeling like a calculated attack. But David's desperation wouldn't allow him to let go, to see the whole truth. "Please don't disappear again. I don't want to feel like I'm—" He cut himself off, unsure of what he was about to say.

Carter made his irritation clear. "I'm sorry, okay? What do you want me to say? But I'm back now. So can you stop second-guessing all the time and can we just...*move forward?*"

"Hawke hasn't been in touch with me." Desperation and accusation mixed in David's voice. "What do you want me to do? Just push it all to the side? Forget what's going on with Sarah because you've just decided to reappear again?"

There was silence for a moment. Carter let out a groan, as if David's voice was tiring him. As if David was asking too much of him. Then he spoke again, his soft tone sounding like a well-polished lie. "No, David. I'm not asking you to forget. I'm asking you to pull yourself together. If you keep holding on to this, it's going to break you." He lowered his voice. "I don't want you to lose your mind over this, okay? You've got to be strong. We all have to be strong. You're not the only one dealing with stuff."

"How can I be strong, Carter?" David's voice was quiet. "But I'm not the only one repeating myself, am I? You are, too, aren't you? You keep saying you can't handle my misery. But you always manage to come back somehow. You aren't really *done* with me, are you?" David was not really sure where his words came from, but they felt true, and they hung in the air as Carter tried to calculate what he would say next.

When he answered, his tone was still smooth, but with something hidden in the layers underneath it. "The reason I came back is because you're my friend, David. But you're making me regret it. You're pushing me away with all this bullcrap."

Something *wasn't right.* David understood that. But he still couldn't come to grips with it. He still didn't know what was going to unfold.

"Okay," said David, his voice barely above a whisper. "I'll stop pushing you away. But…you can't fool me, Carter. I know there's something going on that you're not telling me."

The call ended there, abruptly. David's fingers trembled as he tried to imagine the consequences of his words.

During the next few days, Carter kept calling, checking in more often. Each time he spoke it felt more like a performance, rather than a genuine act of friendship. His words sounded reassuring, but they were hollow. David voiced his suspicions again, but Carter dismissed them.

"I was drunk that night," he would say. "Stop imagining things, man. You know how it is when you're drunk. I didn't mean to say half those things. Stop holding on to it, let it go. We're in this together, we can do this. It's always been you and me. *Always.*"

But David couldn't shake the sense that something was wrong, no matter how hard Carter tried to reassure him. Sarah's warning about the "tax man" had woken something up inside him. No matter how cool Carter seemed, there was always too much distance in his words, and David had the sense he was being manipulated. David had become aware, but he couldn't confront his awareness. If he did, he would feel like a fool, a string-puppet. Whatever the truth was, it kept slipping away, making David drown in paranoia. Carter's constant bombardment of reassurance replayed itself like a mantra in his mind. *"It's all in your head."*

For days, David tried to push away the relentless feeling that something was wrong. He desperately tried to cling on to the idea that Carter was his friend, but it was obvious that Carter was frustrating him. From the beginning, from the first day Sarah went missing, he'd made him feel worthless

The part of Sarah that was still alive in his heart had opened a door in his mind, and through it, he was coming closer to the truth – a truth that he'd been too confused to believe before, a truth that he had barely been aware of: that he was a pawn in a darker plan. A long, drawn-out, sinister game.

In particular, he felt that the fishing trip felt strange when he recalled it. It felt like a surreal attempt to recreate older, simpler moments. Carter had planned it as a "getaway," an opportunity to "relax and clear your head." As if they could just pick up from where they'd left off after Carter had displayed his disgusting behavior. The fishing trip had been planned to make everything seem normal again. Carter's words were carefully crafted, each gesture calculated. He examined David's reactions as if he were a test subject. David understood this now, he had cracked the code, and he felt more alienated than ever.

Carter had barged into David's life. Sarah's disappearance was chaos, and he had injected himself into that chaos, like a needle infected with HIV. His presence was never comforting. Carter was a force – he was always there, always observing and reacting to reactions. David's confusion and pain were something to laugh about. It was all gaslighting – which David remembered he had admitted to, but he'd twisted it into a dark joke, claiming that since what he was saying was true, it couldn't be considered gaslighting. But nothing he'd said was true. It was all deliberate manipulation, designed to make David question his entire reality.

David remembered how Carter had made him suspect he was a federal agent or a government official, trying to pin Sarah's death on him, but then withdrawing that proposal when he admitted to being guilty, creating even more doubt and haunting uncertainty. Carter smirked at David as he fueled his paranoia, making him feel like a person on the verge of a full mental breakdown.

Carter's behavior was sickening. Feeding on David's vulnerability, distorting his sense of reality to the point where he couldn't distinguish whether Carter was real or a figment of his imagination, only existing to torment him psychologically at a time when he was shaking in fear for his wife's safety.

And then had come the turning point, when David snapped in the living room, attacking Carter, begging him to leave him alone. Carter had laughed, egging on his rage and despair. Then, something had shifted. Carter, causally and offhandedly, claimed he would return to David's life with more empathy. His words were strangely comforting, and David had foolishly believed them. He allowed himself to trust Carter again; he let his guard down, as if everything was going to magically reset, like pulling a lever could fix someone's personality – it was an undeniable lie, a pure illusion. And then, Carter had proved himself to operate through a hundred small wounds inflicted on David, with the promise that he was the only one who could heal them. This created a morbid form of bonding between the two, which David could not understand or see through, causing him to get caught in Carter's spider's web again, and again, and again.

But now, David was waking up. He understood this wasn't about *healing*. This wasn't about *friendship*. It was about how long Carter could play his game, how long he could keep David dependent. Keeping David in the dark, always. Questioning himself, questioning what was real. But after everything – the emotional cruelty, the gaslighting, the empty promises – David now understood. Carter was a psychopath and a predator, someone who thrived on constant control. And David had only now figured out he was the victim.

It was all a bad trip. With every interaction, Carter had been manipulating him from the start. Everything Carter had done was a maneuver carefully constructed to keep David needing him to verify what was real and what wasn't. But Carter never provided him with an answer; he would just get off on David's weakness and confuse him even more. But now, with the help of the angel in his heart, with the help of the words of Sarah's memory, David had seen through the cracks in Carter's façade.

He felt sick. He wanted to scream and shout at Carter, to expose him for what he was. But he was still unsure how to break free. How do you escape from someone like that? His paranoia was telling him that Carter could be dangerous. And that if he tried to escape or expose him, he would face dire consequences, even perhaps his own death. The very thought of Carter shot fear through every vein in his body.

David's phone buzzed again. It was Carter. David's hands trembled as he clicked the green button to answer the call.

Carter's presence in his life was a constant reminder that he could not escape the web he was trapped in. Paradoxically, David told himself it didn't matter anymore. The truth had been discovered. So, he answered the phone, ready to face Carter with a newfound power: the power of truth.

"David?" Carter's cool and controlled voice slid through the phone.

David hated him. There was no fake empathy in Carter's voice now, no warmth, only a sadistic emotional distance. "What is it now, Carter?"

"There's something important I have to tell you." Again, it sounded rehearsed. "It's about Sarah."

David froze. Carter sounded certain about something. *Too certain.* The missing piece of his life, of everything that had gone wrong, was about to be revealed.

"It's better if we talk face to face. At your house. There are some things I can't tell you over the phone."

"Have you found her?"

"David. We'll talk when I'm at your place. The answer to that is yes, we found her. But I can't reveal anything else just yet. Please let me come over and explain things to you face to face."

There was a darkness in Carter's tone that became pure fear in David's mind. It took him a while to unfreeze; the shock had locked his body in a state of panic, where he couldn't run or fight. So, gripped by fear, all he said was, "I'll be waiting for you here."

After the call ended, David stared at the screen for a long time. He felt like this was the moment everything would come crashing down. He tried to prepare himself mentally for the worst, but he was terrified. He wasn't sure if it was Carter that scared him, or if his thoughts were now too close to the terrible truth. It pulled him into a pit of doubt, and all he could think about was the abyss, the void he entered from time to time, where anything was possible, where all information was destroyed – keeping the truth shrouded in darkness.

Carter was on the way, and there was no way of knowing what hell he'd bring with him.

David paced up and down in his shoddy little living room. The brakes in his mind had stopped functioning, and it raced with hundreds of scenarios, none of them comforting at all. The moment when everything would change was rapidly approaching, and his heart thudded loudly inside his chest, pumping the blood rapidly to his head, making him feel weak and nauseous.

He waited for the ring on his doorbell. Carter seemed to be taking forever, even though only a few minutes had passed. But David was sure about one thing: the news Carter was about to bring with him would be something far darker than he had ever anticipated. He felt it, deep in his bones, after hearing his serpentine voice on the phone.

Finally, the doorbell rang. David heard the soft rustle of Carter's shoes on the welcome mat. He opened the door, and there he was, standing right in front of him.

Carter made his way to the living room. His presence made the room feel suffocatingly small. David tried to brace himself; as if he were sitting on the seat of an airplane with a broken turbine heading straight for a crash, he tried to ground himself, but none of it worked.

Carter had come in carrying the same smirk that David loathed. He even recognized the claustrophobic sensation David was feeling, and did the honor of making it even worse by closing the front door completely and shutting all the windows so no fresh air could enter the room, which would also keep what he was about to tell David safe from any potential eavesdropping neighbors.

His detached, calm and predatory demeanor made everything worse. David couldn't bring himself to speak. His mind raced with the gas pedal pushed down full throttle, but all he could extract from his thoughts was: *How could any of this be real?*

Carter did not allow David to start asking questions. Like a razor-sharp blade, his voice sliced through the silence effortlessly but violently. "So, have you been wondering about the suitcase? The suitcase that was found in the trunk of your car?" Carter knew David's brain couldn't process the words, so, lightly and playfully, he continued. "You didn't know? How the tax department got it all figured out in the end? David, the tax department has a pretty tight system." Carter's eyes were bright with a sick amusement. "Once someone can't pay their taxes, and they seize a vehicle, it's sent to a secure lot, it's catalogued and parked there by the IRS Asset Seizure Unit." He paused to let the words sink in. "Your Ford Tempo was parked there inside a row with other seized, crappy little cars, all of them with their case number tagged on them. But something was different about yours." Carter could see that David's heart was about to leap out of his throat. "One of the workers, Ben – he's a sharp kid, too smart for his own good – he noticed something. A smell." Carter leaned forward, right into David's face, their noses mere inches apart. David could smell the whiskey on his breath. "A smell that couldn't be ignored. At first, Ben thought it was either gasoline or dust or grit or something building up in the cars. But then it got more pungent, more foul. So, he walked around the place, trying to find out where it was coming from. And when he got to your Ford Tempo...well, let's just say it didn't take him too long to figure it all out."

David wanted to stop listening, to shut Carter out, to run away and forget this entire nightmare. But his body couldn't move. The words kept coming at him, faster than he could process.

Carter was overjoyed to watch David struggle. Even if he was a man without empathy, he could still calculate what other people were feeling, while staying cold and detached himself. "They opened up the trunk," he said as if he was talking about something trivial. "They found a suitcase. The smell coming from it – disgusting. The unmistakable smell of decay. Someone had tampered with the suitcase, of course, sealing it as best as they possibly could, even putting locks on it. But the fabric was bulging, and yes, that was enough to tell them something wasn't quite right. They managed to open it up. They found Sarah. Well, what was left of her, at least." Carter was still casual, as if he was talking about the weather. "She was fresh enough, but bloated. Discolored, like a blue-green kind of color. Poor Ben couldn't stomach it. The first thing they could do was run the prints. They took the fingerprints left all over the suitcase, ran them through the system, and guess what they discovered?"

David didn't want to know, he could already hear Carter's next words before they were spoken.

"The fingerprints were yours, David." A dark satisfaction filled Carter's voice. "Every single one. They were all over the suitcase."

David began to sob, harder than he ever had before. He was literally screaming into the void.

Carter helped him stand up and gave him a spider-like embrace, as if wrapping a fly in his silk. Then, holding on to his victim, he began to giggle. Something about that giggle didn't make sense. And he was about to reveal why.

CHAPTER 12

David couldn't believe Carter had the audacity to giggle like that after what had just been said. "What – what the hell is so funny? Are you sick in the head?"

Carter released him, pushing him back with a little force, as if discarding a kill he couldn't even be bothered to feast on. His demeanor remained calm and cool as usual. "Let's go sit at the kitchen table, I have something that you may or may not find relieving, which I need to admit to you."

"What more is there to hear?" asked David, disgusted and angry. He felt violated.

Carter had to literally guide him to the kitchen table and sit him down. He sat down opposite. "Now, this may come as a good or a bad shock, for reasons I'll explain soon. But the whole story about Sarah being found in your trunk…Guess what, David? I made that all up."

"What…what the hell are you talking about? Does that mean she's alive?"

"Yes, David. She's alive. And I know where she is. You see, the reason she's missing? It's because I kidnapped her. She is now gagged and bound to a chair in a secure location, under the watchful eyes of a guy I call Big Mike. He's part of the syndicate."

Carter quickly put his briefcase on the table and opened it. He slapped on two rubber gloves and pulled out a Colt Python revolver. He aimed it straight at David's head, making it clear he was not allowed to make any sudden movements.

Carter continued talking, his voice dripping with venom. "Guess what, David? Hawke is part of the syndicate, too. The gun he found at Golden Gate Park? He planted it there. He planted half your fingerprint on there, too – we retracted it from the coffee mug you'd been drinking out of whilst you and I spent many pleasant times together, talking about Sarah's meaningless life. It was pure dumb luck that half of your print matched with an ex-serial killer's. Oh, we were so excited. We paid off the guards to turn off the CCTV and let us into his holding cell so we could give him the cyanide capsule. Then we blackmailed him, told him he was going back to jail one way or another, and of course, that gave him the motive to do what he did.

"But here's another little secret. It was Hawke himself that carried out the executions of all those prostitutes. Just to cause chaos in the city, just to make things feel a little more terrifying for you, but mainly, because the syndicate gets off on the suffering of others. And because of his knowledge of forensics, he could cover everything up.

"And now it's you and me, sitting opposite each other. Are you ready for what's about to come next?"

Carter pulled out his cell phone and dialed Big Mike. He placed the phone in the middle of the table and waited for Big Mike to pick up. Sure enough, he did.

"Mike, I need you to speak as loud as you can so this impotent idiot sitting across me can hear you. Ungag the bitch and let her talk, too."

Big Mike had to raise his voice quite a bit so his words could be heard, but Sarah's screams were more than audible to David. They made him feel as if he was being stabbed in the stomach repeatedly with a blunt object.

"We can hear you loud and clear, boss!" yelled Big Mike. "Hey Sarah, I think the boss wants you to talk to your idiotic husband! What have you got to say?"

"David! David!" This was the first time David had heard her real voice in what felt like a century, and the pain inside her screams completely obliterated what was left of him. "He's going to ask you to do something, they've had it planned for a long time! Please, darling. Don't listen to him! Save yourself! I'm begging you! Always remember, I'll love you until the end of time!"

"Mike, gag that bitch again. She's talking too much."

Big Mike did as he was asked, muffling her cries, and then Carter returned his attention to David. "You want to know another little secret, David? Remember all that talk about having kids? Well, guess what? She's three and a half months pregnant!" Carter started giggling again, showing off his poisonous, wet smile.

David's world collapsed on itself. He was being ripped limb from limb by Carter's cruelty. The revelation that Sarah was still alive yet beyond his reach felt like an amputation without anesthesia. He couldn't process the emotions flooding into his worn-out, destroyed, tormented soul. Each passing second became more agonizing than the last, like his entire nervous system had caught fire and was burning hotter and hotter. He had lost everything, even his unborn child.

"Why are you doing this, Carter?" he found the courage to ask.

"*Twelve thousand dollars overdue.*"

Carter had said it so many times, yet David only now knew why. But it wasn't a realistic motive for wanting to do this to someone's life; so, David realized that, even now, even so close to the end, Carter still wouldn't give him the truth. His real motives? David couldn't imagine them; they would remain a mystery forever. All he knew was that Carter was acting as who he was – the worst thing that could ever happen to someone's life.

When Carter was finally satisfied that David knew what he was, he began to speak again. "Chloroform. That's how I managed to kidnap her so easily. I put a towel soaked in chloroform over her face, she went limp, and I used her car to drive her to the location she's in now. But enough of the nitty gritty, David – I'm about to give you a hell of a proposal. Are you ready for it?"

David said nothing. He just stared back at Carter with fear and pain in his eyes.

"I can see from the expression on your face that you are fully ready to accept the gift I am about to give you. So, let's play.

The gun I have in my hand is a Colt Python revolver. It has the capacity to fit six bullets in its cylinder. You will do the honors of loading it with these." Carter menacingly lined up five bullets on the table between them. "Now, I'm going to hand over this gun to you, but don't be a smartass and get Sarah killed before she's had a fair chance to survive, Big Mike is still listening to this whole conversation over the phone. The game we are going to play is simple. You take that gun and you point it to your head. You pull the trigger. If by some miracle there is no bullet in the chamber, I let you go and I let Sarah go, and you can continue with your lives, and I'll be out of your lives as quickly and as abruptly as I came into them. But if you pull that trigger and you die, we kill Sarah as well. We'll probably be able to frame someone else for your deaths – as you know, we've got Hawke on our side – or, if that's not possible, we'll probably blackmail someone into admitting to it. Either way, we're covered. If you refuse to play the game, we kill both you and Sarah anyway.

"Oh, and by the way, when I told you not to be a smartass, I meant if by any chance you even think about pointing the gun at me and pulling the trigger, well, number one, I wouldn't care, because I wouldn't be alive to care, and number two, we'll kill both you and Sarah even after you've managed to kill me, because you don't know how deep my network goes.

"So, what's it going to be, David? Do you want to pick up this beautiful revolver and give it a try?"

David's mind raced through every possible way out of this situation. But there was only brutal inevitability; there was no possible escape. The Colt Python, waiting so eagerly to be picked up by him, was the only way. It was his only option. If he refused to do as Carter asked, Sarah and his unborn child would die, and he would die, too. Carter had planned things too meticulously, his web stretched out vaster than David could imagine, neutralizing any attempt to turn the game in David's favor.

David's rage wanted him to make Carter pay. But his heart told him that if he tried anything drastic, Sarah would suffer.

He focused on that one-in-six chance, that one chamber in the revolver that could possibly be empty, and if he was lucky enough, it could save them both.

He spent a moment to look up from the Colt Python and back into Carter's predatory eyes, and he made up his mind. He accepted his fate.

His hand trembled as he reached for the revolver, the weapon that had the power to decide it all. His fingers fumbled around for the bullets Carter had lined up on the table and nervously loaded the weapon.

Then, with a sudden surge of courage, David spun the cylinder, pointed the gun to his head, and pulled the trigger.

AUTHOR PROFILE

My name is James Fischer and I was born in 1995. I've been passionate about storytelling since childhood, inspired by the thrillers and fantasy novels I devoured in my early years. While I don't weave fantasy into my own writing, I do explore contrast—whether in personality dynamics or shifting mental states—a theme that plays a central role in *The Tax Man*.

My background in English Language and Literature, alongside my fascination with psychoanalysis and philosophy, shaped my approach to storytelling. While academic frameworks taught me structure, I wanted to preserve the essence of literature, blending personal insights with the themes that intrigue me most.

In my time as a trainee accountant, I witnessed the chaotic world of bureaucracy firsthand—an experience that fueled the creation of Carter, a character who blurs the lines between psychopathy and bureaucracy.

If you enjoy dark psychological thrillers with deep character explorations, I'd love to hear your thoughts! Leave a review and let me know how *The Tax Man* made you feel. Also do stay tuned for my upcoming books for some more mind-bending journeys into human nature.

Publisher Information

Rowanvale Books provides publishing services to independent authors, writers and poets all over the globe. We deliver a personal, honest and efficient service that allows authors to see their work published, while remaining in control of the process and retaining their creativity. By making publishing services available to authors in a cost-effective and ethical way, we at Rowanvale Books hope to ensure that the local, national and international community benefits from a steady stream of good quality literature.

For more information about us, our authors or our publications, please get in touch.

www.rowanvalebooks.com
info@rowanvalebooks.com